SHOWDOWN

'YOU TALK REAL BIG FOR A SMALL MAN. NOW EITHER BACK IT OR APOLOGISE.'

There Slinger had it, the small Texan was calling the play. He would not back down, nor would his partner. So Slinger took notice of the situation. He was backed by two good men, any advantage of the light was with him, and he knew how fast he was. There was only one thing to do now.

'WE'RE WAITING, SMALL MAN,' the blond giant said softly.

Speedy Slinger started his move. Hands making their lightning grab which had brought him victorious through several of these affairs. Even as his move began, the rest of the room broke into sudden action.

Books by J. T. Edson
Arranged in chronological order of stories

29. COMANCHE

Civil War Stories

30. THE FASTEST GUN IN TEXAS
58. KILL DUSTY FOG!
21. THE DEVIL GUN
63. UNDER THE STARS AND BARS
26. THE COLT AND THE SABRE
1. THE REBEL SPY
35. THE BLOODY BORDER
62. BACK TO THE BLOODY BORDER

The Floating Outfit Stories

4. THE YSABEL KID
56. ·44 CALIBRE MAN
64. A HORSE CALLED MOGOLLON
50. GOODNIGHT'S DREAM
51. FROM HIDE AND HORN
THE HIDE AND TALLOW MEN†
21. THE HOODED RIDERS
12. QUIET TOWN
11. TRAIL BOSS
37. WAGONS TO BACKSIGHT
48. TROUBLED RANGE
52. SIDEWINDER
20. RANGELAND HERCULES
17. MCGRAW'S INHERITANCE
38. THE HALF-BREED
44. THE WILDCATS
2. THE BAD BUNCH
HELL IN THE PALO DURO†
54. THE FAST GUN
43. CUCHILO
THE SOUTH WILL RISE AGAIN†
9. A TOWN CALLED YELLOWDOG
41. TRIGGER FAST
46. THE TROUBLE BUSTERS
25. THE MAKING OF A LAWMAN
28. THE LAW OF THE GUN
42. THE PEACEMAKERS
SET A-FOOT†
57. THE RUSHERS
47. THE FORTUNE HUNTERS
7. THE HARD RIDERS
14. THE RIO HONDO KID
16. WACO'S DEBT
3. THE TEXAN
34. THE FLOATING OUTFIT
55. APACHE RAMPAGE
8. RIO GUNS
60. RIO HONDO WAR
40. GUNSMOKE THUNDER
45. THE MAN FROM TEXAS
32. GUN WIZARD
36. THE SMALL TEXAN
31. THE TOWN TAMERS
53. RETURN TO BACKSIGHT
27. TERROR VALLEY
15. GUNS IN THE NIGHT

Waco Stories

24. SAGEBRUSH SLEUTH
5. ARIZONA RANGER
37. WACO RIDES IN
6. THE DRIFTER
DOC LEROY M.D.†
49. HOUND DOG MAN

Calamity Jane Stories

33. COLD DECK, HOT LEAD
18. CALAMITY SPELLS TROUBLE
19. TROUBLE TRAIL
22. THE BULL WHIP BREED
10. THE COW THIEVES
61. WHITE STALLION, RED MARE
13. THE BIG HUNT
THE WHIP AND THE WAR LANCE†

John Slaughter Stories

59. SLAUGHTER'S WAY
SLAUGHTER'S NEIGHBOURS†

Waxahachie Smith Stories

65. SLIP GUN†

Rockabye County Stories

THE PROFESSIONAL KILLERS
THE ¼ SECOND DRAW
THE DEPUTIES
POINT OF CONTACT
THE OWLHOOT
RUN FOR THE BORDER
BAD HOMBRE†
THEY CALL IT PROGRESS†

† In preparation

and published by Corgi Books

J. T. EDSON

RIO GUNS

TRANSWORLD PUBLISHERS LTD
A National General Company

RIO GUNS

A CORGI BOOK 552 07891 3

Originally published in Great Britain
by Brown Watson, Ltd.

PRINTING HISTORY
Corgi Edition published 1968
Corgi Edition reprinted 1969
Corgi Edition reprinted 1972

This book is set in
Georgian 10/10½ pt.

Corgi Books are published by Transworld Publishers, Ltd.,
Cavendish House, 57–59 Uxbridge Road, Ealing,
London, W.5.

Made and printed in Great Britain by
Richard Clay (The Chaucer Press), Ltd., Bungay, Suffolk

For Bob Molloy,
My Oldest Fan

CHAPTER ONE

AZUL RIO TOWN

RENE HAMILTON looked through the window of the stage coach at the town of Azul Rio, New Mexico, and wrinkled her nose with distaste. The adobe and wood-built structures lining the street were not what she would call home. Until very recently home to her meant an oak panelled Tudor house in the hunting county of England's Leicestershire. This town, even though it was, according to her friend and travelling companion, Gloria Knight, the county seat, did not impress her.

Still it was to be her home now. Her father was partner in a ranch in the Azul Rio basin. She was joining him after the death of her mother in England and was going to live out here. Gloria, sitting by her side, had met her in New York and travelled with her overland, first by train, then stagecoach.

They made a contrasting couple as they sat side by side on the hard and bumpy seat of the coach. Rene was a tall, willowy blonde, her hair taken back in severe style, her beautiful face pale and aloof. She was wearing a black riding habit which would have looked far more in place at a fox hunt meet in Leicestershire than out here on the wild plains of New Mexico.

If Rene did not look to belong out West, Gloria certainly did. She was a product of the range country and the Azul Rio basin was her home. Except for the last few years at school in Atlanta she'd been in the West all her life. She was not as tall as Rene, her red hair fluffy and loose. There was not the classic beauty of Rene about her face, but it was a warm, friendly and pretty face. Her rich, full curves strained against the old, tartan shirtwaist and brown levis she wore. On her feet, the levis cuffs hanging over them, were a pair of high-heeled, fancy stitched boots.

The coach came to a last jolting halt before the Wells Fargo office. The guard vaulted down and opened the door, holding out his hand to help Rene. Around the front of the office, awaiting the mail, was a crowd of local citizens. Gloria swung down smiling; these were all acquaintances and the women would want to discuss the latest fashions from the east with her.

Then the warm and welcoming smile died. The women looked at her, nodded greetings and turned away quickly. The crowd did not even wait for the mail but moved away.

'What the hell?' Gloria muttered half to herself. She could never break herself of the habit of talking to herself when she was worried.

Rene glanced at Gloria, a smile coming to her face. From the first they'd got on very well together. Gloria was different now she was in the West. In New York she'd been shy, quiet and indecisive, but once they'd reached Dodge City she became happy, confident and completely at home.

Looking around, Rene could not see anyone who might be her father; she'd not seen him since she was eight and wondered if he had changed.

'Will papa send retainers to help us?' she asked.

Gloria turned her attention back to her friend, smiling back even though she was worried by their reception. 'Well I thought pappy and Uncle Mike might be here to meet us, or send some of the crew along. But don't you go calling a cowhand a retainer, he just wouldn't appreciate it.'

At that moment a tall, wide shouldered young man rode towards them, his big black horse moving easily under him. Gloria looked him over with interest for she was Texas born and Texas men always interested her. He was looking at them and making right for them.

The man was handsome, his face tanned, his black moustache trimmed just enough to be tidy without being too fussy. From the expensive black Stetson on his head, through his tidy looking range clothes, down to his boots with the Kelly spurs on the heels he was Texan. A cowhand who took good care of his clothes and bought good clothes in the first place. It was the mark of a tophand.

Gloria glanced at the clothes, then at the gunbelt around the man's waist. It was a rig she'd heard about but never seen before. The holster hung on a longer flap than was usual, the walnut butted Colt Cavalry Peacemaker's seven and a half inch barrel showing its foresight through the open bottom. The holster was cut so the trigger of the gun was left clear for a purpose. This was what was known as a halfbreed rig, the user did not even draw his gun for the first shot, merely swivelled back the butt of the gun and fired while still in leather. It was a rig which was not much used, but if a man used it he was good.

The young man swung down from his horse, removed his hat and came up to the girls. 'Would you be the ladies for the KH?'

'Why sure,' Gloria agreed.

She knew her guess was right. The man was Texas, yet his soft, even drawl was deeper south than the Lone Star State. One did not need a printed sign to know he'd learned his trade in Texas, not when he rode a double girthed saddle and his leatherwork was decorated with a star motif. Yet she was even more sure he was deeper south than that.

'Your pappy sent me along to collect you. Ole Brazos was driving the buggy but one of the team threw a shoe and he's stopped off at the blacksmith's to get it fixed.'

'Why didn't pappy send along two of the old boys to fetch us?' Gloria asked. Brazos was one of her old friends but she did not know this man. 'You're new around here, aren't you?'

'I'm not old around any place, ma'am.' The young man's eyes were on Rene as he replied. 'The name's Smith.'

'Just Smith?' Gloria inquired, amused by Rene trying to remain aloof and disinterested in the true British fashion.

'Yes'm. How'd you guess?'

Gloria glanced at the man, he was smiling and she realised there was more to the words than first met the eye. 'Guess what?'

'That I'm Just Smith.'

'You look like you might be Just Smith. Rene, this here's Just Smith from Texas, although I'd bet it was lil old G'o'gia afore that.'

Rene looked at the young man for a moment, then held out her hand to him as Gloria finished the introductions. The man was one of her father's employees apparently, although his manner was not that of a hired hand. However, she knew conditions were different in America and she was willing to conform to the ways of the land. Gloria accepted the man so it must be all right to unbend. He certainly looked presentable enough and there was nothing but politeness in the way he shook hands with her.

'You called it right, Miss Gloria,' Just Smith went on to Gloria. 'I'm from Texas, but it was Georgia before that.'

Rene could see the young man was more interested in her than in Gloria and felt vaguely uneasy. Gloria was also uneasy but for a different reason. That name, Just Smith, it struck a chord somewhere but she could not just remember where she'd heard it before. She knew he was from the deep south and not from a poor family either. There were many of these southern boys moved as a result of a shooting scrape too many and were now among the top names of the gun-fighting fraternity. Glancing down Gloria saw the way his hand hung negligently near the butt of his gun. That was no pose taken for their benefit, he stood that way naturally.

'Why didn't pappy send along two of the old boys?'

'Three years is a fair time. Most of them retired, there's only Brazos left of the old crew.'

That figured when she came to think about. KH's old hands would have become stove-up and too old for the hard, exacting work of cattle herding, and retired. If all the crew were of the same standard as Just Smith there would be no need to worry about the future of the ranch.

Just seemed anxious to change the subject. He glanced around, along the length of Azul Rio's main street then turned to the girls again. 'I reckon you could use a meal before we leave for the ranch.'

'I certainly could,' Rene spoke for the first time, as she too looked along the street. It appeared to be made up of businesses only, stores, a couple of saloons, the county offices and jail spreading on either side of the trail. Opposite the stage station was a white, adobe building with a wooden sign above the door, reading, 'Henery's Eating House and Bathrooms.' 'Is there a restaurant in town?'

'Henery's place there,' Just answered. 'It might not look up to New York standards but the food's good.'

Rene was not sure of the propriety of eating with a hired man but did not argue. The fresh air and the bumpy ride had given her an appetite far beyond any she could ever remember. If eating with Just Smith would get her a meal she did not mind. Somehow she guessed his social graces would not embarrass her, for like Gloria, she guessed his background was far more than a hired man.

'Lead on, Mr. Smith,' she said.

'Why sure. ma'am. One thing though.' Just watched the girl for any sign of disapproval, ready to stop if he saw it. 'Out here if you call a man mister after you've been introduced it means you don't like him. I'm Just to my friends.'

'Very well then, Just. I'm Rene.'

Gloria watched the other two start off across the street, a smile playing on her lips. Rene was catching on fast and would make the grade out here. She followed them, glancing at the three horses which stood at the hitching rail. They were horses to catch the eye, a paint, a blood-bay and a white. Not one of them stood less than seventeen hands, each had a low horned, double cinched saddle, with a bedroll strapped to the cantle, a rope fastened to the horn and a Winchester in the saddleboot.

'They'd make a real mount for a man,' Just remarked, stopping to look the horses over. 'I reckon I'd best tie this old hoss of mine away from them, that white looks mean enough to eat it.'

While Just was taking his horse further along the trail, the two girls studied this trio of magnificent animals. Rene was a fine horsewoman and could see the breeding in the horses. Gloria was looking as one who knew the west. She guessed the three horses belonged to Texas men but did not go around to look at the brands. Such curiosity was against Western ethics.

Just tied his horse then came back to the girls. He pushed open the batwing doors of the Eating House and allowed the girls to enter first. Gloria looked around the room, she'd been here many times before. It was not changed since her last visit, the same dozen or so tables, each with a clean cloth and four chairs. The same paintings on the walls and the same two doors at the right side of the room, marked 'Gent's' and 'Ladies Bathroom.' Opposite the main doors, at the other end of the room was a door leading to the kitchen. Henery, the owner of the eating house, came through this as they entered.

Business was slack this morning, only two of the tables being occupied. At the far table, next to the kitchen door, sat two obvious dudes. At another, two Texans sat face-to-face with each other. They would be the owners of two of those horses out front. Then from the door marked 'Gent's Bathroom' came the sound of a man singing 'Barbara Allen' in a pleasing tenor. The words of the song interspersed with splashes and gurgles. He would be the third Texas man.

Henery advanced towards the newcomers, his fat face beaming. Gloria smiled back. It was good to see an old friend again. He looked, as always, like a fat cherub, but Gloria knew he'd broken up three attempted hold-ups here. The last time he'd left two of the would-be robbers dead on the floor.

Henery came to a halt, then for an instant the smile died as he recognised Gloria. It came back again fast but she'd caught the worried glance he exchanged with Just Smith. There was something wrong, she could feel it in the air.

'Why Miss Gloria, this is an unexpected surprise,' Henery greeted, he bowed over her but did not appear to be completely at ease.

'Howdy Henery, I'm pleased to be back. Meet my friend, Rene Hamilton. She's come to stay.'

Once more Henery inclined his head. His bearing was more in keeping with the headwaiter of some fashionable cafe in the East. He looked at the blonde girl, then at Gloria, and once more that worried expression flitted across his face.

Rene was satisfied with the cleanliness of the place and looked for a menu on the table. The problem of ordering was taken out of her hands by Gloria who spoke with the air of one who knew the menu off by heart.

'We'll take son-of-a-gun stew followed by nigger-in-a-blanket, then coffee. Three times.'

Henery turned and departed without another word and

Rene looked at the two smiling faces facing her. 'Whatever is that you ordered?'

It was Just who explained. 'Son-of-a-gun stew's made from the choice pieces of calf. Cook throws all he's got on hand into the pot with them and boils the lot until you can't tell what anything is. The other is a dessert made out of dough and currants.'

Gloria sat back listening to Just as he went on to tell Rene about Western food. Her attention went to the two young Texas men sitting two tables away, finishing their meal. The one with his back to her was very tall; even seated she could tell that. His hair was a rich, golden blond and curly. His shoulders were wide. straining the expensive tan shirt which was obviously tailored for him. He tapered down from the great spread of shoulders to a slim waist and brown levis trousers. Around his throat was knotted a tight rolled scarlet silk bandana and about his waist a wide, hand-carved buscadero gunbelt. It was a gunfighter's belt, the ivory butted Colt Cavalry Peacemakers showing their trigger guards from the cutaway lips of the holsters.

The second man, facing Gloria, was smaller. not more than five foot six at most. Like his friend, his expensive JB Stetson hat hung on the back of his chair, low crowned, wide brimmed and Texas style. His hair was a dusty blond colour, curly and looking as if it had just been washed. His face was young looking and handsome at first glance. Gloria gave it only a glance for alongside the other man he was insignificant and would hardly be noticeable. Yet for all of that, had Gloria looked closer, she would have seen it was a strong, intelligent and powerful face. The grey eyes flickered at Gloria, meeting hers for a moment, then returned to his friend once more. She glanced at the tight rolled blue bandana round his neck and the dark blue shirt. He did not appear to be the kind who would own such a fine horse as any of that trio out there.

Henery returned with a tray, balancing it with a casual grace and ease which told of long practice. He set out the food before the girls and Just laid out the knives and forks, then withdrew once more. In the bathroom the singer changed to another song and the splashes ended. Rene looked down at the well filled plate and took up her knife and fork. Before she realised what she was doing she'd eaten all the stew and looked up at the smiling faces of her friends.

'The ride must have given me an appetite,' she remarked, looking at her empty plate.

The dessert followed and Rene ate with a will. The ride in the stage was enough to give anyone an appetite. Then with the coffee on the table she saw Just Smith sitting back in his chair and said, 'You may smoke if you wish, Just.'

Taking out his makings Just rolled a smoke with deft fingers. Gloria decided now would be as good a time as any to get to know what was happening here in Azul Rio. The welcome at the stage station and Henery's worry were enough to tell her all was not well.

'Have you worked for the KH long, Just?' she asked.

'Three months or so now. Came in for the spring round-up and stayed on after it was over.'

'What kind of work do you do, Just?' Rene put in before Gloria could frame her next question.

'Ride herd, anything that comes up. I could show you a lot easier than tell about it. When we get out to KH I'll take you out and show you, if you would like that.'

'I certainly would.' There was eagerness in Rene's voice which brought a smile to Gloria's lips. It was good to see her relax and unbend; she would get on all right out West now.

The doors of the Eating House swung open and a small, dirty and ragged Mexican boy entered. He stood hesitantly at the door for a moment, then crossed the room. Hat in hand he stood before the table looking from one to the other, finally he bowed to the table in general and spoke in a rapid flow of Spanish. Gloria listened, finding her Spanish still as good as ever. The smile died from her lips as the little boy spoke, she sat erect and her eyes went to Just Smith.

Dipping a hand into his pocket Just threw the boy a coin and snapped a couple of words to him. Turning, the boy scuttled from the room, the batwing doors swinging to behind him. Just sat back, not speaking for a moment although he could see both the girls were interested in what was said.

'The button says he put your gear on the sidewalk outside the stage office. I'll go along to the blacksmith's shop and tell ole Brazos to pick it up on the way out of town.'

'That wasn't all he said.' Gloria's face was grim. 'I speak Spanish as well as you do. Who's Lanky Kline and why did you kill him?'

CHAPTER TWO

SPEEDY SLINGER

RENE gave a low gasp as she stared at this tall, handsome and pleasant spoken young man. She looked down over the table at the butt of his gun then slowly back up at Gloria. It was hard to believe her ears, but she knew Gloria would not be joking about such a thing.

'Why'd you shoot him, Just?' Gloria went on.

'He rode for Lanton's S Star. I found him on KH land branding S Star on a KH calf. He went for his gun and I had to kill him.'

Gloria felt relieved. The killing was completely justified by Western standards. A cattle thief was shot on the spot, or hanged if taken to trial. 'Who's this Lanton, he wasn't here when I left.'

'He's the new boss of the S Star. Formed the Azul Rio Cattle Syndicate along with the Flying P, Lazy F and Estrades. KH is the only ranch not in it. The Syndicate's been importing gunhands and looking for trouble. I didn't want to say anything about it until your father'd seen you.'

'You mean a range war?' Gloria asked.

'Not yet. That was the first trouble we've had with them. It could shape that way if the S Star pushes your pappy much more.'

It was then Gloria could see the reason for her cool reception when the stage arrived. The people of the town, scenting trouble in the air, would not wish to show friendship to either side. Then she remembered Rene was not a Western girl and turned to explain something to her.

'Don't get the wrong idea about Just. He killed Lanky Kline to save his own life. The other man would have killed him if Just hadn't shot first.'

'I realise that,' Rene's voice was cool, neither panic nor dislike of Just Smith showing in it. 'Papa wrote and warned me of the rough land out here. I'm sure Just was justified in shooting.'

Just Smith could hardly believe his ears. He'd expected the English girl to be afraid of him. She looked at him, her eyes meeting his with no flinching or loathing.

'What happened after the shooting?' Gloria asked. 'The little boy didn't sound as if he liked Kline.'

'Pepe didn't. Kline used to bully him. Your pappy told Lanton and the sheriff what happened and warned them any other rustler would get the same. That didn't set well with Lanton or his tame sheriff, but they haven't made anything of it so far.'

'Tame sheriff?' Gloria inquired, for the sheriff of Azul Rio County was an old friend of the KH.

'Sure, Sam Coulter was found dead over on the S Star, Flying P line. Looked like an accident. Then Lanton got this hombre Lynch put in. Made it real cosy for S Star from the start.'

Hooves sounded outside as three riders came to the Eating House, halting their horses and swinging down. Seated facing the door Just Smith stiffened slightly and Gloria looked out under the batwing doors. The men appeared to be looking at Just's horse, then tying their own horses to the rail they came on to the sidewalk. The batwing doors swung open and the men entered. halting just inside.

To Gloria's eyes, even though they wore range clothes, the three men were not cowhands. They had a look about them, the look of paid killers, men who sold their guns to the highest bidder. This was true of the two tall men who flanked the small man in the centre. It was far truer of him. He was small. not much over five foot four she guessed. His clothes, from the low crowned Stetson hat to his boots were costly, but they were not the clothes of a hard-working cowhand. His face was pale with a pallor that did not speak of long hours of open air work. Around his waist was a gunbelt and in the holsters pearl handled Colt Civilian Peacemakers.

Just Smith read the signs, and knew what this trio were

doing here. Quickly he slapped his hands palm down on the tabletop in the rangeland sign for a truce. Almost imperceptibly the small man nodded in agreement and Just jerked his head in a signal which Gloria interpreted correctly.

'Come on, dear,' she shoved back her chair. 'Let's go and red up.'

Without giving Rene a chance to object Gloria took her by the arm and led her towards the ladies bathroom. Opening the door Gloria gently pushed the other girl inside, following her and turning to make sure Just got an even break.

The three men were advancing, the smallest moving with dainty and cat-footed grace. His hard, cold black eyes never left Just's face, his hands brushed the butts of his guns.

'Well, well,' he said with well simulated pleasure. 'If it ain't the Texan who shot down poor ole Lanky.'

'Sure Speedy,' the man at the right agreed. 'And after you telling that he'd got to stay clear of you. He even took your place at the hitching rail out there.'

'He's looking for trouble. Speedy,' the other agreed.

'Go move his hoss, Sam,' the small man ordered, his eyes still on Just's face.

Just Smith's mouth drew to a tight line, his chair scraped back as he came to his feet. To move another man's horse was an unforgivable insult. From the corner of his eye he saw the two Texas men looking on, the taller swinging round in his chair. Yet Just held his temper down. He was not afraid of the small man, even though Speedy Slinger was S Star's top gunhand. One thing was holding him back from taking up the challenge. He was under orders to fetch the two girls back to KH and he did not want any shooting while they were with him.

'I'll move it myself,' the words were torn unwillingly from his lips.

'I told you he was yeller, boys,' Slinger hissed. 'Real yeller, and him saying he beat Lanky in a fair fight.'

'Ole Lanky was fast. Near as fast as you, Speedy. And that yeller rat tries to make out he killed Lanky in a fair fight,' the gunman at the left went on. 'If it was fair it makes Smith near as fast as you.'

'And he ain't. He murdered old Lanky and tries to say Lanky was a thief. Show's he's yeller, way he's backing down right now.'

'I'll come back after——' Just began, his face reddening as he fought to hold down his temper.

'You're yeller, Smith,' Speedy Slinger was not even looking at the two young men who were watching everything. 'You're like all the other damned, lousy Texans, yeller as——'

Two chairs crashed over. The two Texas men were on their feet now. Gloria got her first look at the tall man's face and the small man's armament. The face was as handsome as she'd ever seen, and reminded her of photographs she'd seen of classic statues of Greek gods. The small man wore a buscadero gunbelt, white handled guns butt forward in the holsters.

'Mister,' it was the smaller of the pair who spoke. 'When you call down this gent here it's private. When you take in the rest of us Texans it becomes personal.'

'Shy out, both of you,' Slinger warned, his voice savage. 'This is a private fight.'

'Mister,' the blond giant replied. his voice deep and showing breeding. 'You've gone past all privacy right now. The remark you made calls for some apologising.'

The air was suddenly charged with deadly menace. It exuded from the three hired killers but more so it came from the two soft talking young Texas men. It was then Gloria realised the small man was there. Suddenly he was more than there, he dominated the others with his presence. Speedy Slinger also realised that he was up against the real thing now. This was no pair of dressed-up boys, but were men born in the land, well able to handle themselves in any man's fight.

'Reckon you don't know who I am,' he said, not wanting an added complication on his hands. 'Do you know what they call me?'

'Not unless it's Shorty.'

Slinger's lips drew back in a snarl. He was very conscious of his lack of inches in this land of tall men. To have that small, insignificant looking cowhand call attention to the lack made the insult far worse. His hands lifted the cover

over the pearl butts of the guns and his voice dropped to an angry hiss.

'I've killed men for saying that. My name's Speedy Slinger and they don't call me it because I drink my likker fast.'

'Maybe because you talk fast?' the small blond asked. 'You start in to apologising.'

Gloria felt relieved now. She knew the three men who must be from the S Star meant to force Just into a fight and kill him. With this intervention there might be no trouble even now. She knew why Just did not fight and admired him for it although she knew he would return to answer the insults as soon as he'd delivered them safely to the KH. It was then she caught a movement from the corner of the room and looked to where the two dudes sat. They were watching everything, hands under their coats.

'Apologise to you?' Slinger sneered. There was no chance of bluffing the two young men out so he was set to fight. 'I'll handle you when I've fixed this other lousy Texan.'

'You talk real big for a small man. Now either back it or apologise.'

There Slinger had it, the small Texan was calling the play. He would not back down, nor would his partner. Slinger was no fool, he knew why Just Smith did not fight. It was not fear that held the KH hand back. So Slinger took notice of the situation. He was backed by two good men, any advantage of the light was with him and he knew how fast he was. There was only one thing to do now. Kill Smith as intended and get those two Texans who put their bill into the game.

'We're waiting, small man,' the blond giant said softly.

Speedy Slinger started his move, hands making their lightning grab which had brought him victorious through several of these affairs. Even as his move began the rest of the room broke into sudden action.

The small blond's hands crossed in a sight-defying blur of movement, his matched, white handled guns coming out ahead of any other's. Flame tore from the muzzles of the guns held, waist high and centring on Slinger. The bullets struck even as the little killer's own guns were coming clear of leather. Even as Slinger was hurled backwards by the smashing impact of ·45 lead, the tall blond's guns were throwing bullets into the man who'd stood at Slinger's right.

Just Smith was fast with a gun, but he was not in the same class as those two Texas men. His hand dropped, gripping the butt of his gun and tilting it back, thumb easing back the hammer. Even as the muzzle of the gun lifted, still in leather, he fired, the bullet ripping into the shoulder of the third man, spinning him round. The gunman hit the batwing doors and staggered out through them. He gripped the reins of his horse, tore them free and managed to mount the horse and light out of town at a dead run, heading across the range.

The two dudes were on their feet in the corner of the room, each now held a short barrelled gun and was bringing it into line on the three Texas men. Gloria opened her mouth to scream a warning but she was too late. Her help was not needed. The men's bathroom door was thrown open and a tall, black-haired, dark young man erupted. He was naked to the waist and his feet were bare but he held an old Colt Dragoon revolver in his right hand. He took in the situation even faster than had Gloria and roared out, 'Dusty!'

One of the dudes reacted fast, coming round with his short barrelled gun cracking at the newcomer. The dark young man dropped even before the shot was fired, his old Dragoon gun booming louder than a cannon as he hit the floor. Gloria gave a gasping cry. She had never seen a man hit in the head with a round, soft lead ball from one of Colonel Sam's four pound giants. It was not a pretty sight. The head seemed to burst open on the impact, the dude's body stood erect for an instant then crashed down. Gloria turned back into the bathroom, her face ashy grey and her stomach heaving.

The small blond came spinning round faster than a lizard hunting for cover. He dropped to one knee as he turned, right hand gun coming up and lining, bucking back in the palm of his hand even as the second dude's bullet passed over his head, so close it stirred his hair in passing. The dude jerked under the impact of two hundred and thirty grains of lead. His gun fell from his hand, he spun round and dropped.

Then there was silence in the room, the powder smoke wafting and blowing away. Speedy Slinger and his man were down, the two dudes still in the corner, their gun-trap, laid for Just Smith, smashed without even closing.

The man whose timely appearance saved the small blond came to his feet. He was tall, but without the great spread of shoulders of the blond, yet there was a whipcord strength about him, and his dark frame was scarred by bullet and knife wounds. His long, curly hair was so black it almost shone blue in the light, his face innocent and young looking with red hazel eyes which were neither young nor innocent. He looked down at the bodies, then with a casual shrug, turned and walked back into the bathroom once more.

In the women's room Gloria recovered a grip of herself, and found Rene holding her and looked up. 'It was terrible,' she gasped.

'Yes dear. Is Just all right?'

'He's all right. Stay here. I'll tell the sheriff what happened, when he comes.'

Rene shook her head. 'No dear, this is concerning both of us.'

'Sure, but I saw what happened and can explain it. I'd like to keep you out of it. Please, for me.'

With a smile Rene agreed, her every instinct telling her to go out and stand by Just, but she knew she might say the wrong thing and make matters worse. So she stood back and watched Gloria walk out of the room and shut the door behind her.

Henery came up, his face pale. He glanced at the doors of the Eating House and listened to the sound of approaching people. 'I saw it all, Miss Gloria. I'm willing to testify Just did all he could to avoid a fight.'

'Thanks Henery. I'll keep you out of it if I can.'

A fair sized crowd was gathering in the building by now, men and women crowding forward to look at the bodies and talking amongst themselves while looking at the Texans who were loading their guns and ignoring the chattering townspeople. Before Gloria could get to Just and the two Texas men there was an interruption. A man was forcing his way through the crowd, pushing them aside arrogantly. He was big, heavily built, his face coarse. brutish, the eyes piggy and small, the nose reddened by either long hours in the sun or looking at the full glare of an open whisky bottle. His store clothes looked more expensive than a sheriff of a small New Mexico county should be able to afford. His gunbelt was an expensive gunfighter's rig, but he did not have the look of a skilled man with a gun.

Gloria glanced at the two men whose intervention saved Just Smith. The taller glanced at her, then half a smile flickered on his lips as if he recognised her, or thought he did. She was sure she should know him but could not believe her luck if she was right.

By now the sheriff was through the crowd. He was about to speak when he stopped dead. His eyes went first to Just Smith, then down to the bodies. The change in him was almost ludicrous, it was almost as if he knew what to expect here and just been given a bad shock.

'What come off here?' he asked, looking down at Slinger's body again.

'Man got to damning Texas and died of it,' there was disdain in the small Texan's voice as he watched the play of expression on the sheriff's face.

The sheriff stiffened, thrusting forward his badge slightly to emphasise his position. 'Who killed Mr. Slinger?'

'I did.'

'Cut a rusty?' the sheriff asked, looking at the soft talking, insignificant young man, then at the others.

The mildness seemed to fall away from the small blond and there was a subtle difference in his voice as he replied, A badge doesn't give you that much license, mister. The man allowed he was some fast and went to try and prove it. He died of a case of slow. You think I didn't play fair, say so. The right way.'

Behind the sheriff there was a stirring amongst the crowd as they prepared to get out of the firing line, for he was known to be a bad man when crossed. However, whatever his faults Sheriff Lynch was no fool. He was not a good gun himself but knew many who were. This small Texas man was as good as he'd ever seen. Who the pair of Texans were

Lynch did not know. He did know they were the equal of any of the S Star hired. He could see that Slinger died in a fair fight. Slinger was too slow to match the guns of this soft spoken young man from the Lone Star State. One thing Lynch knew was that this put the Texan in a far higher class than he intended to monkey with.

'No offence, mister. It's only that Slinger was faster'n most,' Lynch was ingratiating, his voice oily and, on the surface, friendly.

'Not fast enough,' the tall blond put in.

Lynch chose to ignore that remark and turned his attention to Just Smith. 'That's three in a week, Smith. Mr. Lanton isn't going to like this.'

'I mourn for Mr. Lanton,' Just replied. 'And it ain't three but five.'

Without even looking at the bodies in the corner of the room Lynch replied, 'They ain't S Star men.'

'Now how'd you know that, sheriff?' the small blond put in. 'You never even looked at them.'

'They ain't cowhands,' Lynch looked flustered, realising he'd made a bad mistake there.

'Nor are Slinger and his pard,' Just snapped. 'S Star doesn't hire a cowhand, only guns. I didn't want trouble today or any other time. You said three in a week. Lanky Kline was putting S Star on a calf with a KH mammy.'

'Which same's again the law, they do tell me, sheriff,' the tall blond's tones were sardonic and he glanced at Gloria again. 'Leastwise it is down home to Texas.'

The sheriff's hands moved from near his gun butt, the fingers working stiffly. He chose to ignore the big man's remarks and once more spoke to Just Smith. 'You tell your boss I ain't having any more killing in my balliwick. You're too handy with your gun.'

'Man has to be. You tell Lanton the same thing.'

Clenching his fist, Lynch growled, 'One more crack like that'll buy you a pistol whupping.'

Just smiled bleakly. 'Any time you feel like it whup ahead.'

The sheriff was once more compelled to revue his actions. He knew Just Smith was handy with a gun. Lanky Kline had been no slouch and he went under in a fair fight. That put Just Smith almost in the same class as the two Texans there or Speedy Slinger. It was a class the sheriff did not intend tangling with unless he was full backed by at least half a dozen deputies. Before he could speak again, a tall, leathery old-timer came through the batwings. He halted by the sheriff's side, hand on the butt of the old Spiller and Burr cap and ball revolver in his holster. Looking down at the body he gave the wolf howl of delight.

'I knowed it. I knowed all along ole Just here could handle that short growed misfit there,' he whooped in Lynch's ear. 'Now the boy's gone and proved it.'

'Easy Brazos,' Just barked, for he knew the old timer would take a lot of pleasure in annoying the sheriff.

Before Brazos could say any more the door of the men's bathroom was opened and the third Texan made a more leisurely appearance. Now he was fully dressed, a black Stetson on his head, black bandana, black shirt. In fact the blackness was only relieved by the walnut grips of his old Colt Dragoon, laying butt forward in the holster at his right side and the ivory hilt of the James Black bowie knife at his left. For a moment he stood at the door, then advanced to stand by his two friends. He looked at the sheriff with hard, sardonic and mocking eyes.

'You bunch work for KH?' Lynch asked, knowing Lanton would wish to be informed if the KH was hiring three such hard and handy looking young men.

'Don't know about this gent here.' the small blond once more spoke for the others. 'We don't, we're only passing through on our way to Texas.'

Lynch gulped, he did not like having to ask the next question, but he knew he must. 'No offence meant, mister. But just for the record, who are you?'

The small blond smiled, and indicated the tall, handsome blond. 'This is Mark Counter. This is Loncey Dalton Ysabel—'

Again Lynch gulped, his face working under the strain he was feeling. Those two names meant something to him. 'Then you're——!'

'That's right, mister,' there was open mockery in the black dressed boy's soft said words. 'He's Dusty Fog.'

CHAPTER THREE

JUST SMITH EXPLAINS THE TROUBLE

DUSTY FOG. The word, soft spoken, ran through the crowd and everyone knew how Speedy Slinger came to die. Dusty Fog, segundo of Ole Devil Hardin's mighty OD Connected ranch in the Rio Hondo country of Texas. Leader of Ole Devil's floating outfit, two members of which were with him right now. Dusty Fog, a name that ranked with Wes Hardin, King Fisher and Bill Longley as an exponent of the art of triggernometry. A name which ranked with Charles Goodnight, Gil Favor and Stone Hart as a trail boss. A name which ranked, in the war when he rode as a cavalry captain at seventeen, with Turner Ashby and John Singleton Mosby as a raider in the finest Dixie tradition. That was Dusty Fog, the small, insignificant man, the Rio Hondo gun-wizard who might go overlooked in times of peace but never in war.

Mark Counter, the tall, handsome blond was a rangeland dandy, yet still a tophand and if anything even better with cattle than Dusty. Mark was known as the Beau Brummel of the range country, his dress dictating cowhand fashions throughout Texas as once it was copied by the bloods of the Confederate Army. Mark was known as a skilled bare-hand fighter yet his skill with his Colts was hidden by Dusty Fog's. If Mark had ridden alone his skill would have been better known, for Dusty said Mark was at least the second fastest man he knew.

The last of that trio, the Ysabel Kid, was a legend in his own life-time down on the Rio Grande. He was still discussed by U.S. and Mexican Customs officials as a one boy crime wave, even though it was several years since he retired as a smuggler. He was the son of an Irish-Kentucky father and a Comanche-French Creole mother. From each of these breeds he gained something invaluable. From his father came a love of fighting, the sighting eye of an eagle and the ability to handle a rifle with almost magical skill. From the Comanche came his horsemanship, the ability to read sign and follow tracks where others would be lost. From the French Creole strain came his love of cold steel and the skill with his bowie knife which would have gladdened the heart of old James Bowie himself.

These were the three men who stood facing Sheriff Lynch, faces showing no expression, eyes unfriendly. Lynch was pleased he did not have his three deputies with him, that gave him a good excuse not to make any further moves against the Texas men.

'All right,' Lynch turned to the men who stood around. 'Some of you lend a hand to get the bodies to the undertaker's.'

Some of the crowd moved forward, lifting the bodies and carrying them out of the Eating House. The rest of the crowd hung around, waiting in the hope that there might be some fresh developments. They all saw Lynch was in a tight spot, for they knew he owed his post as Sheriff to the good offices of Lanton. This could put Lynch in an awkward spot, for Lanton would expect him to make something of the killings. There was little he could do unless he could shed some light on the fairness of the fight. He wanted to do this but not at the risk of his own skin.

'Were there any witnesses to the shooting?' he asked.

Gloria saw Henery open his mouth and shook her head. She did not want him involved in this and knew it might go badly for him if he did get involved. She stepped forward, glancing again at Mark Counter, wondering if he recognised her. 'I saw it all. Just Smith was in town to meet me.' For some reason she did not want to let the sheriff know about Rene. 'We came in here for a meal, then Slinger arrived with two men. They tried to force a fight on Just but he took it. Then they insulted Texas which brought Mark and Dusty into it. Slinger made his play first and Dusty coppered it. Mark got the other gunman and Just wounded the third. Those two dudes tried to cut in and the Kid stopped them. When the smoke cleared Speedy Slinger just hadn't made it at all.'

Mark grinned at the girl, winking, but she kept her face straight and expressionless. She met Lynch's gaze without first flinching, her eyes on him making him look away first. Lynch did not like this, for he wanted to try and make the girl look a liar, but knew if he tried he would have Smith, the three Texans and the crowd against him.

'Who might you be?' he growled.

'Gloria Knight. Just works for my pappy.'

The sheriff knew that here was a chance to discredit Gloria's statement on the grounds that she would be biased in favour of her father's man. To do this would mean facing the wrath of those young cowhands and that he did not mean to do. He glanced at the three again then asked, 'Is your pappy taking Cap'n Fog at the KH?'

'Why shouldn't he?' Gloria countered.

Lynch could see he was going to get nowhere with the girl. 'How did them two dudes get into it?' he asked.

It was Dusty who answered. 'Way I read it they were working for, or with Slinger. They were there either to take a hand if Just here was too much for Slinger, or to say it was self defence when Slinger killed him.'

'If anybody got round to asking was it Just here got killed,' Mark went on, looking pointedly at the sheriff. 'It sets just like a guntrap from where I stand.'

'But they didn't work for the S Star.'

'So you keep telling us,' Dusty replied, his tones mild yet mocking. 'I still don't see how you know that without going close enough to see.'

'That's a fool question,' Lynch said moodily. wishing he was away from here, away from those grey eyes which seemed to bore right through him.

'It's a real good question, friend,' the Ysabel Kid made his last word sound anything but friendly. 'Happen a man looks long enough he can turn up a real smart answer to it.'

Lynch's hands clenched. He was not used to being treated in this way for he was known to have the backing of the S Star. However, he knew the Ysabel Kid gave respect only where it was merited and no amount of hired guns would make him change his manner. He knew that unless he got away from here fast he would lose even more face and endanger his position here in town. Turning on his heel he growled at the crowd, telling them to get about their business, watched them leave, then turned and followed. He did not look back, but his face and ears were red as the batwing doors swung closed behind him.

Henery came over to Gloria, shaking his head worriedly. 'This will cause trouble, Miss Gloria. I am willing to go into a witness box and tell the truth about what happened here.'

'I know that,' she replied. 'But I don't want you getting mixed up with this if we can avoid it. Thanks Henery. Just, I'll get Rene and we can head for home.'

Mark watched the little girl walking towards the bathroom door and remarked, 'I remember when I was a button back home, there used to be a red-haired lump of perversity, fat as an Arkansas Christmas shoat. come to see us. Took her hunting one time and she caught a skunk. Don't allow she ever got over it.'

Gloria swung back, her face lighting up with a smile as she ran to throw her arms round Mark's neck and kiss him. 'Cousin Mark!' she whooped. 'I thought you'd forgotten me.'

'Why?' Mark replied, holding her back at arm's length and looking at her. 'Do you reckon I go around winking at strange gals?'

'If you don't I'd surely be surprised.'

Mark laughed, introduced her to his friends then went on. 'I wasn't sure you recognised me. Of course I know I'm a whole lot better looking now, having grown up all tall and handsome.'

'I wouldn't say that. I used to like you in that lil ole velvet suit and with long curls hanging down your shoulders.'

Mark saw his two friends giving him speculative glances as they heard this blatant falsehood and spluttered out an angry denial. Before Gloria could think up any more disparaging details, true or false, the old timer interrupted.

'Huh, goes round kissing near strangers and forgets an ole friend like me. It——'

'One thing for sure,' Dusty put in. 'That gent who hired

those guns won't be forgetting his friends any. One of them got away wounded, leave us not to forget. He left town like he was going someplace.'

'And that someplace could be home,' the Kid went on, with hope rather than worry in his voice. 'Likewise sending back some help, mebbee.'

'So the sooner we see ole Redtop here back to her pappy the better it'll be,' Mark finished.

'I got the buggy outside,' Brazos remarked. 'We can head out when you all finished whittle whanging.'

'All right.' Gloria felt joy in her heart. The three young Texans were going out to the KH with her. If there was trouble they would be a tremendous asset. 'I'll fetch Rene and pull out.'

Returning to the bathroom Gloria found Rene standing at the part-opened door. The English girl's face was paler, aloof and yet there was no sign of either panic or hysteria on it. Her voice was cool enough as she asked, 'Is Just all right?'

'Sure, it's all over now.'

'Didn't the sheriff, or whatever you call him, arrest Just?'

'No. Just shot in self defence. He didn't kill any of the men. He tried to avoid the fight. Rene. Those men were out to kill him.'

'I realise that. I know Just would never kill unless forced to do so. I also know that if a man wears guns he may have to use them. Who are the other three men who helped Just?'

'The tall one's my cousin, Mark Counter. The other two're his good friends. The small one is probably the fastest man with a gun alive. But they's all like Just. None of them would draw on a man unless he was forced into it. They're going to escort us to the ranch. Do you mind?'

Rene's hand dropped lightly on to Gloria's head, ruffling the hair gently, a smile on her face. 'I don't mind. It will be safer for us. Would it be all right to thank them for helping us?'

Gloria hugged the other girl, looking up at her. 'You're all right, Rene. Just like your pappy. But don't bother to thank them, they don't appreciate kindness. Come on, we're going home.'

The two girls left the bathroom and crossed to the waiting men. Gloria introduced Rene, then led the way out of the Eating House. There was a fair crowd lounging around but no one said anything as the party went to the horses. Brazos was last out, glancing at the buggy, then at the cowhorse fastened to it.

'Can you still drive a buggy, Glory gal?'

'Why sure,' Gloria went past the buggy seat and unfastened the horse, swinging into the saddle. 'And ride a hoss, too.'

Brazos grunted something about the danged females of today having no respect for age or dignity. Rene, aware the Texans were giving her approving glances, came alongside Just. On an impulse she took his hand and gently squeezed, their eyes met for an instant. Rene's cheeks were flushed as she accepted Brazos' hand to help her into the buggy. She watched the three young Texans take their horses, Dusty mounting the paint, Mark the bloodbay, then the Ysabel Kid gripped his saddlehorn and vaulted up astride the big white. There was something wild and alien about the way he did it which made her wonder what sort of man he was.

Brazos started the buggy team moving forward and the men formed up around it, riding easily in their saddles. They stopped at the stage station to collect the girls' baggage, loaded it on to the buggy, then went on again, leaving the town.

Lynch stood in the door of the jail and watched the party leaving. One of his deputies standing by him grunted. 'They don't look so much at all. I could sing any of them to sleep.'

Lynch grunted, his mouth twisted in a sneer. 'Any one of them could take you and think nothing of it. Get your hoss and head for S Star. Tell the boss what happened to Speedy. Tell him KH looks to have three new hands.'

Gloria sat on her horse with ease and grace, she looked at Just Smith, then at Brazos and could restrain her curiosity no longer. 'What's it all about, Just?' she asked.

'It's not for me to say, Gloria.'

'I'd rather leave it for your pappy to tell it. All right, I'll tell you what I know, which same isn't much. Like I said, I only came in for the spring roundup and stayed on. Lanton was already here, been here about six months before that. He bought up that old S Star, brought a partner in with him who took on the Lazy F. The partner's name is Santone but he doesn't talk or act Texan. He's a mean, shifty eyed hombre, Lanton's big and hawg fat. They've got upwards of forty men working for them although there is barely enough for half that many. They don't do much range work and I reckon they'd be better with a gun than a rope. Kline was like that, I don't know if Lanton told him to steal KH stock or not.'

'That all of the S Star bunch?' Gloria went on as Just stopped.

'Well, Lanton formed what he calls the Ezul Rio Cattle Syndicate. He got Painthoss from the Flying P to join. Painthoss's boys are all right. They're hands from the Pecos mostly, but a good bunch and don't mix with the S Star guns. Then Miss Estradre's joined up with the Syndicate since her father went down into Mexico for a vacation.'

'Estradre! You said Juanita Estradre joined the Syndicate?' Gloria snapped. 'Why Neety and I are like sisters, she's grown up with me. She wouldn't go against us.'

'Well, she's been and gone and done it,' Brazos growled. 'Allus said you can't never trust a greaser.'

'Juanita's no greaser, you flabby jowled old goat,' Gloria yelled. 'She's Spanish Creole and her ancestors were Conquistadores. She wouldn't go against me.'

Brazos grinned. His little gal hadn't tamed down while she'd been in that Eastern school. 'Waal, she's done it. She's with Lanton near on all the time now, and what I say still goes. Why, when I rid with Old Devil Hardin in the Mexican——'

'If this is about Uncle Devil and the Mexican War it's probably all a lie,' Dusty interrupted, ignoring the spluttering Brazos and turning to Just who was riding alongside Rene. 'What's the trouble, isn't there enough land or water to go round?'

'Sure, there's plenty of water and land in the Azul Rio

basin for the four spreads. There always has been,' Gloria put in.

'Lanton's a landhawg. He wants all the range around here in his hands and the KH won't have it any,' Just went on.

'What's a rangehog?' Rene inquired, for most of the conversation was going over her head.

'It's a disease.' Mark answered. 'Affects some men.'

'Sure,' the Kid agreed. 'And there's only one cure for it.'

'What is that?'

'The old one, ole Colonel Sam's point forty-four cure.' The Kid's voice was mild and deceptively innocent. 'When a man gets landfever the only cure is to kill him.'

'How bad's the trouble?' Dusty asked.

'Just been talk at first. We did start to lose some stock but I put a block on the game. The hands out at KH aren't fighting men and they won't stack up against gunmen. Won't be many of them stand if it comes to shooting. The KH don't run much to fighting men these days.'

Gloria snorted. She could read the tone in Just's voice. 'Just Smith. I might be fresh back from the East but I'm nowhere near blind. I could see you straining back to stop ramming Slinger's words down his throat. You only held back because Rene and I were there. Backin' down like that was probably the bravest thing you ever did.'

'I saw it that way myself, amigo,' Mark agreed.

'Sometimes it takes more courage to back down than to stand and fight,' Dusty went on. 'You did the right thing there, Just.'

Just Smith felt as if a great load lifted from him. He'd been worried how those three fearless fighting men, Dusty Fog, Mark Counter and the Ysabel Kid, regarded him. He was sure they thought of him as a coward, who was only willing to fight when given powerful backing by better men. He was also worried about how Gloria regarded his actions, worse, how Rene must feel about his killing men. Now he could see the three Texans and Gloria had read the correct motives behind his actions. He looked at Rene, his hand still tingling from her gentle touch. There was no sign of either revulsion, or fear in her eyes. She understood him.

'Hell,' Brazos grunted, anxious that his young friend should be seen in the best possible light. 'Ole Just here ain't scared of nothing. You mind him. Cap'n Fog? From the Concho River sheep war.'

'Drop it, Brazos!' Just snapped, for he was not proud of what happened in the Concho River trouble.

The three young Texans looked at Just Smith with fresh interest, for they'd heard of the trouble down there in the Concho River country of Texas when sheepmen tried to move in on the land the cattlemen tamed and cleared of Indians, Mexicans and badmen. Just Smith's name was mentioned as one of the leading lights of the deadly, gunsmoke-ending feud. They also knew he did not wish to discuss it, particularly while Rene was there.

Gloria knew that whatever else Just Smith might be he was a fighting man from soda to hock and he would back up the KH until the last chip was down. If there was to be bad trouble with Lanton's S Star such a man would be invaluable.

'How many of the hands will stick by us, Just?' she asked.

'Brazos, me and a young Englishman called Brit. He's a real nice young feller and all man, stands full sixteen hands high from where I am. The rest won't stick.'

'That's tall odds, friend,' Mark said softly.

'We could likely even them down a mite though,' the Kid went on.

Dusty did not speak for a moment, but looked at the other two. Mark and the Kid were as close as brothers to him and he knew they loved to get into a good fight. Mark was kin to Gloria and that meant he would want to stay on and help the KH out of their trouble. There was little of importance in the Rio Hondo for a time. The floating outfit was being capably handled by Dusty's cousin, Red Blaze, young Waco and Doc Leroy, all of whom were well able to run things in his absence. Mark, the Ysabel Kid and himself would not be missed for a few days and in that time the trouble might come to a head here. He looked at Gloria. The girl was true range-bred and would not panic if there was shooting. The English girl also looked cool enough, not the kind who would get hysterical. Yet they would need help if Lanton brought his hired killers into a full scale war on the KH.

He made his decision as always without asking the others to share in it. 'Reckon your pappy could take on three hands for a spell, Miss Gloria?'

CHAPTER FOUR

KH LOSES HANDS

For a moment Gloria did not speak but there was a wild elation in her heart. If Lanton was pushing for a range war KH could use the very able assistance of the three young men who rode with her. Dusty Fog was known as a master tactician, and the fastest gun in Texas. The other two were equally respected for their fighting abilities.

'Well,' she finally stated. 'The cook's shy a louse and the wrangler wants a nighthawk, so we can take you and Mark, Dusty. But we haven't a thing we want smuggling across the border so I can't see that there'll be a thing for the Kid to do.'

The Ysabel Kid was loud in his protests that he was now a retired smuggler and an upright and honest citizen. Dusty let his friend carry on for a spell then interrupted. 'What do you think. Will your pappy be able to take us on?'

'Sure, there's some work round the spread that only needs a strong back and weak mind.'

'You trying to get out of your chores again, redtop?' Mark asked.

Rene watched the men, then looked at Gloria. The buggy bounced and jolted over the rough trail towards the KH. The trail was hardly more than a series of ruts cut by the wheels of the KH chuckwagon and the hooves of horses headed for town. It did not make for a comfortable journey and Rene envied Gloria who was riding astride a cowhorse. Rene herself was a good rider and would far rather have been on a horse than bouncing about on the seat of the buggy.

Looking round her she could see nothing but mile after

mile of rolling range country. The lush, deep grass spread over the land as far as she could see in any direction but she could see no sign of human habitation. After a couple of miles she started to see scattered bunches of long horned cattle. These did not act like the tame bossies she'd been used to. At the first sight of the party approaching, these animals whirled and fled at a speed which made her stare in wonder.

'Are they all strays, Just?' she asked.

'Nope, they're KH stock. We let them rangefeed out here, and don't gather them unless we want a herd for market or the roundup's on.'

'Is this part of our ranch, then?' Rene looked around expecting to see the ranch house somewhere near at hand.

'Why sure,' Just could guess what she was thinking.

'Good lord!' Rene stared at the young man. 'Do we own all this. But where is the ranch house? I can't see it.'

'It's about another three miles, about in the middle of the spread,' Just explained, pleased to be having this chance to talk with Rene. 'It's a fair sized spread.'

'It's enormous.'

'Fair, only fair, by Texas standards,' Gloria put in. 'Why, either the OD Connected where Dusty rides, or Mark's father's R over C are bigger than the average Eastern county. They're so big a regular crew can't handle all the work, they have to use a floating outfit.'

'What's that?' Rene was eager to learn all she could about this new life she was to lead.

'Five or six men who spend their time away from the main ranch. Out in the back ranges. They take a cook along and act like a moving ranch house. Do the sort of work the other hands handle closer to home. The OD Connected use one most all of the time. When we're to home, Mark, Lon and I usually ride for our floating outfit.'

'I've got a lot to learn, haven't I?'

'Why sure,' Dusty agreed. 'I'll reckon ole Just here'll be real pleased to teach you all he can.'

Rene blushed and Just glared at Dusty, the others all looking on with tolerant smiles. Gloria turned to Mark and pointedly asked him about his father. Dusty and the Kid also took the hint and started to talk over a cougar hunt they'd been on back in the Rio Hondo while Brazos concentrated with fierce energy on handling his team. This left Rene and Just free to talk with each other and she started to ask him innumerable questions all about range life and work.

Never in all his life had Just Smith known time pass so quickly. He found himself wishing the ride would never end. The girl was pleasant and he knew she was attracted to him as he was to her. He doubted if her father would approve of him. Hamilton might like and respect him as a cowhand but would hardly like the idea of Rene getting too friendly with a man whose reputation for wearing a fast gun made him the target for other fast guns. Just Smith knew he was the owner of such a reputation. There was little security for such a man.

Rene was watching Just's face and wondering what drove this handsome and cultured young man to the life of a cowhand. She could tell he was well bred and guessed there was more to Just Smith than met the eye.

'Say, redtop,' Mark spoke loudly to Gloria. 'Remember that time we put you on the hoss, back home?' He turned to Rene. 'You should have seen her. She was caterwauling like a cougar on a log. We had to rope her into the saddle to get her to stay on.'

'You got that story the wrong ways round,' Gloria howled back. 'It was you they had to tie on, not me. Anyways, you're still riled because I gave you a black eye for pulling my braids.'

'Being a southern gentleman I couldn't hit a lady.' Mark explained to the others and looked at Gloria as if expecting her to deny it.

She did. 'No, you didn't hit me. You kicked my shins hard, though.'

'I never kicked a lady.'

'You kicked me.'

'So?' Mark grinned at his cousin. 'I still allow I never kicked any lady at all.'

Gloria started in to tell him in no uncertain terms what she thought of him. He let her finish, then told the others how they'd been coon hunting together and how she lost the seat of her pants trying to stop a dog fight.

'You should have seen her riding back home,' he told Rene, who was laughing merrily now. 'She was surely red at both ends when she got there.'

Gloria's face was red, and she tried to think of something equally disreputable about Mark. Failing this she gave an angry yell of, 'Why you nogood, white topped buzzard. My turn'll come. You wait and see if it don't.'

They were coming up a slope now and on reaching the top Brazos brought the buggy to a halt, allowing his team to have a breather. The others rested in their saddles and Rene looked around her. Below, like a map was stretched the Azul Rio basin. As far as the eye could see the rolling well watered range country of the KH, S Star, Lazy F, Flying P and the E ranches.

'Why it's beautiful,' her voice dropped almost to a whisper. 'I've never seen anything like it before. We must be able to see for miles from up here.'

Gloria watched her friend. She always felt the same when she sat up here and looked down over the Azul Rio basin. She leaned over and raised a hand, to a point. 'Look down there, where that small stream goes round behind those trees. That's where the ranch house is. You can see the smoke, look.'

Rene leaned forward eagerly, looking down the slope to what she would call a wood. Beyond this she could see a curl of smoke rising into the air. The smoke filled her with delight, it was her first sight of the KH, her new home.

Gloria decided that she would be able to show the others how the land lay. Her finger pointed to where the Azul Rio slashed and rolled across the range in a huge curve which formed three of the KH boundaries. She indicated the rough rock and brush strewn banks directly ahead. 'That's our west line. The river forms our line with the S Star. You can see the S Star house right over there. Down to the south, where the smoke's rising, is Estradre's. Right out back there, up towards the hills, is the Flying P. Their range goes right back to the mountains. Then where the Azul Rio curves up there forms our line with the Lazy F.'

Dusty Fog, Mark Counter and the Ysabel Kid sat their horses and looked down on the Azul Rio basin. It was a rich and fertile range country, a country capable of supporting four ranches without trouble. Yet one man with a lust for power and land was not satisfied. That man wanted all of this for himself and was willing to kill to get it.

More than the others the Ysabel Kid was studying the range below. He studied it not as a cowhand but in the Indian manner, making a map in his mind. If it came to war he would be far more concerned with riding scout than handling cattle. To ride scout in a strange country he would need to know where the various ranch houses lay. From his careful, Indianwise study he would be able to roam the Azul Rio basin with the same ease he traversed the OD Connected land. He would know how to get from place to place by the quickest and easiest route, would know where he could hide and remain unseen. It was not the Ysabel Kid who studied the range but a Comanche Dog Soldier with an eye for raiding. Before the others were ready to move off he held in his mind a complete map of the area down below.

They moved off again, and as they rounded the bosque then splashed through a ford in the stream, Rene got her first look at her new home.

The house stood some two hundred yards from the trees. It was a white stone building made in the days when labour was cheap and stone was to be had at the cost of a few lives. The KH house was large, and from the look of it the family lived in the front on the first floor, the hands having their bunkhouse and dining room at the rear. The house side was to the trees, its front to the corrals, two of them, only one of which was in use at the moment. A bunch of horses were moving about in the larger. The smaller, with a snubbing post in the centre was empty. On the side of the house away from the trees were a couple of wooden buildings, a blacksmith's forge and the back-house, and to the rear of the house stood a barn.

Two men came from the house and stood on the porch. Gloria removed her hat, waving it around her head. then she turned to Mark. 'Let's see if pappy recognises you.'

Jack Knight stepped from the porch to meet his daughter as she sent the horse racing forward. He was a tall, bronzed man wearing range clothes and with a low-tied Colt at his side. Beside him was another tall man, but slimmer. although just as tanned. Mike Hamilton wore range clothes, yet he managed to give them an Eastern flavour and he was not wearing a gun.

Gloria came down from the horse before it stopped, the impetus of her landing throwing her into her father's arms. She kissed the man, then turned to watch Hamilton going to the buggy to greet Rene. She wondered how they would greet each other, for they had not met for many years.

Just Smith helped Rene down from the buggy and she stepped forward. Hamilton walked up to her, and they stood looking at each other for a moment.

'Well, m'dear,' Hamilton said, taking the girl's hands and pecking her lightly on the cheek. 'You've grown.'

'Thank you, papa,' Rene's voice was just as cool and emotionless. 'I am pleased to be here.'

The others watched in some surprise as Hamilton escorted his daughter into the house. They wondered what sort of people the English were to control their emotions so well. Gloria clearly did not approve of it all and snorted angrily, then eyed her father.

'See you've still got that old shirt on. And you haven't taught Uncle Mike how to act. He hasn't seen Rene since she was a button and that's how he greets her.'

Knight had been so absorbed in greeting Gloria and the pleasure of having her home for good that he did not think of how Hamilton acted with Rene. In fact Knight hardly noticed anything. He paid no attention to the three young men at all. Then he heard the tall blond one remark.

'Say, how'd you reckon a big hombre like that sires such a short-growed filly as that red-haired lump of perversity there?'

Jack Knight swung round, his fists lifting and his face showing sudden anger. He took a step towards Mark, then stopped and a grin came to his face. 'You're Ranse's boy, aren't you? Young Mark?'

'Why sure, Uncle Jack,' Mark agreed, taking the offered hand.

'Damned if you ain't uglier than your pappy ever was, boy,' Knight growled. He was a strong man but that grip made him wince.

'You're just jealous. Pappy told me about all the dance-hall gals he took off you the old days.'

'That's a lie,' Knight roared. 'Ranse Counter never took any dance-hall gals off me.' He caught his daughter's accusing eye. 'He couldn't. I never went in no such places.'

Mark introduced his two friends and Knight looked them over with a speculative gaze. In view of the trouble he was expecting they would be a handy trio to have round. He felt he was having more luck than one man could rightly expect.

'Jack!' Hamilton came from the house fast, his face red. 'Rene told me there was a shooting in town. Some of Lanton's men were killed.'

'Good, who were they?'

Just Smith turned from the hitching rail where he stood by his horse. He glanced back to where Brazos was unhitching the buggy team, then said, 'Speedy Slinger, two more of the guns from the S Star and a couple of dudes they'd got planted to help them out.'

'Did you get them all?' Hamilton asked.

'One lit out wounded.'

'I know you didn't pick the fight, Just.'

'He didn't. Just took more than I would to try and avoid it,' Mark put in. 'They'd laid a guntrap for him.'

'Which same worried me some,' Dusty remarked. 'It was a trap and real well set. Too well for just a chance meeting. Somebody at the spread here let Lanton's men know Just was going to town and where they could find him.'

'How do you mean, Cap'n Fog?' Knight asked.

'The way the trap was set. Those men couldn't have known he was coming to town. They couldn't have known he'd use the eating house, not unless someone who knew where he'd be told them. They couldn't have had the two dudes in the eating house on the odd chance. That's too much coincidence for me. The sheriff acted like he knew what was going to happen too. He was some surprised when he found it wasn't Just laying there.'

'Then you think one of our own men told them?' Hamilton looked with renewed interest at this small, insignificant young man.

'Sure, I don't reckon Just did it. Who'd know about him going?'

'Any of the crew. I went along to the bunkhouse and told

Just to go in with Brazos. It was early last night and any of the hands could have took a hoss and gone over there after,' Knight replied.

'Lon,' Dusty glanced at his friend. 'You'd better cut for sign and find out which hoss was used.'

Before the Kid could move to obey Dusty's orders Hamilton asked, 'What will Lanton say about it?'

'I don't know, or care. It's time KH stopped worrying about what Lanton or anybody thinks. From now on we dig in our heels and hauls down on the rope.'

'That's my pappy talking,' Gloria whooped. 'And I'm right ashamed of you, Uncle Mike. Why you've fought Indians, rustlers and bad whites before now. You're not going to let a bunch of hired guns scare you.'

Hamilton shook his head. 'It's not that, Gloria. But I've got Rene to think about. She's not used to violence and——'

'She's not allowing her father to let down his friends.'

Hamilton turned on his heel and found Rene standing on the porch. Her face was slightly flushed as she saw every eye turned on her. Stepping forward Rene laid her hand on her father's shoulder. It was then she saw the admiration in the eyes of the three young Texas men and knew they accepted her. The feeling gave her more pleasure than she would have thought possible.

Hamilton's hand went up to grip hers and hold it. 'But .... but!'

'Riders coming,' the Ysabel Kid remarked.

The others all turned and saw men riding towards the ranch. They were all cowhands and riding in a relaxed, peaceful manner. The Ysabel Kid had been watching them for some time, and his warning would have come far sooner if there had been any show of hostility among the advancing men.

'Who are they?' Dusty asked.

'Our hands,' Hamilton replied.

'But they should be out with the herd,' Knight went on, his voice sounding angry. 'That's all of the crew except Brit and Lenny.'

The riders came to a halt in front of the house, eight of them. Seven looked nervously at Knight and Hamilton, the other clearly the man in command. He was a heavily built, middle-sized man in dandified range clothes, sporting a pearl handled Remington in a fancy, low-tied holster. He swung down from his horse and came forward, his eyes arrogant. Halting he jerked his thumb back over his shoulder.

'Me and the boys want our pay, we're quitting.'

'Why, Carron?' Knight growled. 'What's the game?'

'They dropped ole Lenny from on that rim above where we're holding the herd. That's why.'

'Get the killer?' It was more of a statement than a question from Dusty Fog.

'Not us, we ain't fighting no war.'

'All yeller?'

Carron looked Dusty over and made a mistake. 'You nervy buttons make me retch. Why you shortgrowed——'

Dusty came forward with a smooth gliding step, the back of his hand smashing up across the bigger man's face with enough force to spin him round. Carron staggered back, snarling a curse and dropping his hand to the butt of his gun. Moving faster Dusty caught the wrist, jerked it up into the air, then down and round. Carron howled, his feet left the ground and he lit down on his back hard. With a roar that was more animal than human he came up and hurled himself at Dusty again, his big hands clawing out to grip the small man.

'Stop him, Mark!' Gloria yelled, for Carron was far heavier and bigger than Dusty.

Mark shook his head, grinning as he watched. Carron might be bigger but he did not know the tricks Ole Devil Hardin's Nipponese servant had taught Dusty Fog. He was going to learn them right now, or Mark did not know his young friend.

Catching hold of Carron's vest Dusty slipped backwards to the ground, his right foot going into the man's stomach. Using Carron's speed and weight Dusty heaved and sent the other man hurling into the air. Carron lit down hard, his gun bouncing from its holster. Dazed and winded he reached for the weapon, then fingers like steel bit into his neck, dragging him erect. His legs were wobbly and he staggered on to the left Dusty smashed into his stomach. Carron doubled over, his face turning an ashy grey colour.

Dusty's other fist drove up, powered by all his weight. The man came erect again and then crashed down on to his back.

'See what I mean?' Mark inquired of Gloria.

Brazos had been an interested spectator. He ambled up with a bucket of water in his hands and dumped the contents over Carron. The man sat up shaking his head, moaning, then dragged himself to his feet.

The other hands looked at each other, then one of them spoke, 'We want our time, Mr. Hamilton. When a nice feller like Lenny gets shot it's time to get out of it.'

'Where's Brit?' Just Smith asked.

'He stayed on. Last we saw he was hunting the man who downed Lenny.'

'And you left him?' Hamilton barked. 'Jack, get their money and pay them off. The sooner they're out of my sight the better I'll be pleased.'

Carron crawled to his feet, bending and picking up the gun. 'Try it,' Brazos said gently. 'That's Cap'n Dusty Fog.'

Carron shoved the gun back into leather, not meeting Dusty's eyes. He followed the other men towards the house. Knight went inside and soon after the cowhands started to come out with their gear, heading for the corral to collect their own horses and ride out. Carron was not amongst the other men and still had not made his appearance when Knight came back to join the others who were talking at the front of the house.

Hamilton watched the men riding away and remarked, 'Well, that's the end of us, Jack. If we haven't brought the herd in by tomorrow the bank will foreclose.'

CHAPTER FIVE

THE HERD

KNIGHT and Hamilton looked at each other, then at the three young Texas men. 'You three wanting a riding chore for a spell?' Knight asked.

'Why sure,' Dusty agreed. 'We'll take on. Mark'll have to head into town tomorrow and send a telegraph message to Uncle Devil and let him know we'll not be back for a spell.'

'You'll want some chow before you head out for the herd,' Gloria remarked, knowing the men would be riding soon. 'Who's cook.'

'Gal called Gloria Knight, she can't be wuss than the last cook we had,' Knight answered, ignoring Brazos' objection to this slur on his cooking. 'You get started.'

'All right,' Gloria remarked, looking at Mark with an expression which boded ill for him, then she turned to Rene. 'You want to be cook's louse, honey?'

'Cook's *WHAT*.'

'Louse, assistant,' Gloria explained.

'Well,' Rene sounded dubious. 'I did learn plain cooking at school, but I'm not——'

'You'll likely improve on ole redtop there's fixings,' Mark put in. 'Her cooking used to be worse than plain.'

Gloria poked her tongue out at Mark, thumbed her nose at him and led Rene off into the kitchen. Dusty watched them go, then turned his attention to Knight and Hamilton.

'About this herd?'

'It's nothing much,' Hamilton replied. 'Three hundred head of white-faces. We needed some money for improvements just before Lanton's man took over at the bank. Took up three thousand dollars on the agreement we'd pay back either the three thousand or three hundred head, or the ranch. The note comes due tomorrow and this new chap will want paying back dead on time. We had the very devil finding three hundred head, they don't survive as well as longhorns, or ours haven't. Aimed to bring in the herd today but we heard Gloria was arriving and so sent the boys to bring the herd in. Meant to go and meet them after the girls settled in.'

'Three hundred head shouldn't take much handling, Uncle Jack,' Mark said, with the air of one who'd help trail three thousand head over the interstate trails.

'They're white-faces, Mark,' Dusty put in. 'And you know they don't trail well at night. We shouldn't have any trouble, there's three of us, the bosses, Just, Brazos and the other hand. We ought to be able to handle them unless there's swimming water to cross.'

'There isn't,' Hamilton liked the way Dusty got down to handling a problem. 'I think we'll take the short way back, Jack. Through that coulee out there. It saved going right the way round.'

The Ysabel Kid suddenly swung round, a low snarl coming from his lips and his face Comanche hard and mean. He went to the corner of the house his hand shooting out and hauling Carron forward. 'You got a good ear, friend,' he said.

'I couldn't find all me gear,' Carron replied.

'Let him be, Lon,' Dusty ordered.

'Why sure,' the Ysabel Kid let Carron loose and stepped back, watching the man heft his bedroll. Following Carron to his horse the Kid watched the man heft the heavy looking bedroll and strap it to the cantle. Then he turned and looked back. The Kid's face was close to him and the soft drawling voice held menace. 'Hombre, happen you stay on round here I'll be on the lookout for you, I'll spit in your face every time I see you.'

Carron tried to meet the red hazel eyes and failed badly. He swung into the saddle and turned his horse's head towards the Azul Rio City trail. Not for a moment did he doubt the Ysabel Kid meant just what he said when he gave that old Texas warning. The Kid would do just that, spit in Carron's face every time he saw him, until Carron either ran or drew his gun.

'Reckon I'd best follow him?' the Kid asked hopefully.

'We need every hand for the herd,' Knight answered. 'Don't you like riding herd?'

'You should like this one, Lon,' Dusty remarked.

'Why?'

'You're always telling me you don't feel natural moving cattle in daylight, so this should set well with you.'

'Why this one?'

'We'll be doing it after dark.'

Knight led the other men through the front door of the house. A hall ran down the centre to the dining-room and the bunkhouse at the rear. At the right was a small office and the kitchen, on the left, windows looking out on the bosque and the stream, was the sitting-room, used by the family on special occasions. The stairs to the bedrooms separated the sitting-room and the men's sleeping quarters. Gloria looked out as the men trooped by. She gave them a look of disgust and asked, 'Were any of you in here a bit back?'

'Nope,' Knight answered.

Gloria looked puzzled. She was sure she'd heard someone moving about in the house. However, she was too busy now to stand talking and let them go into the bunkhouse, as they called the room. The departing hands had left the room in a mess but there was nothing which could not be tidied up. The three Texans took unoccupied bunks and dumped their bedrolls on to their choice, then made their way into the dining-room and sat around the long table. They discussed range matters until the girls arrived with the food.

'Hey shorty,' Mark called, and he pushed away his plate and took up the cup of coffee at the end of the meal. 'This slush looks some weak.'

Rene looked down at her own cup. 'I thought it was rather strong.'

There was a general laugh at this and Hamilton explained. 'Heckling the cook is one of our favourite pastimes, dear. In fact, any cook who did not get swamped with adverse comments on his food starts looking for another job right away.'

'I see I have a lot to learn.'

'Waal, was I you, Rene, I'd surely not let ole redtop there teach you a thing. She'll get it all wrong.'

'You just wait, Mark Counter. Just wait.' Gloria warned. 'My turn will come.'

'Happen it comes before I get back don't keep it,' Mark replied. 'I wouldn't want it at all.'

With the meal over they all trooped out of the house. Dusty, Mark and the Kid decided their horses needed a rest and stripped off the saddles, turning the big stallions loose to graze. Dusty took his rope and went to the corral. He climbed on the rail and dropped inside, looking the horses over as they went by him. A little dun gelding caught his eye as it went by and he waited his time. Shaking loose the rope, Dusty brought the loop up in front of him and to the right. Over his head the loop whirled once, then shot out. With a twist of his wrist Dusty turned the loop so it was flying parallel to the ground and at just the right height. The honda of the rope was slipping, closing the loop, tightening as it fell around the dun's neck.

Mark and the Kid caught themselves a horse each from the remuda, using the hooleyann throw like Dusty. This was the throw always used to catch a horse from the remuda. It was a headcatch and enabled more than one man at a time to catch horses without scaring the rest.

The three young men saddled their horses and swung afork. All three were fighters, and had been picked by men who knew horses for those same fighting qualities.

Once the horses were cooled down and under command again the party rode out across the range. Gloria and Rene came on to the porch and waved to them. Gloria was holding a Winchester carbine under her left arm, and she was to defend the ranch in case of any attack by the S Star while the men were bringing in the herd.

The ride across the range was made with no trouble. It was a new section to Dusty, Mark, the Kid, and they kept their eyes open. In the next few days they were going to travel around this range and would need to know it. About two miles from the house they came to a coulee, a long, deep gash in the land, caused by some volcanic action. It was no more than fifty yards wide and for the most part the banks fell away very steeply. This place was cut to allow an easy way down. At the bottom they turned and rode some thirty or forty yards along and up a natural grade at the other side. Dusty looked round with distaste, for the herd would have to be brought up the other side. The rims of the coulee were brush and rock and covered and would offer good cover if anyone wished to lay for the herd.

There was no time to do anything now, for they were through the coulee and headed on. Then minutes later they saw the cattle, the sun was going down now and the gentle slope opposite them was in deep shadow. The cattle were bedding down, a couple of horses stood, saddled and with reins hanging, but there was no sign of a man.

'Brit's dead too,' Knight growled.

'Looks that way,' Knight agreed. 'Damn those——'

A rifle crashed, the bullet striking in front of them and whining off in a vicious ricochet. They could not see where the shooter was, and not even the Ysabel Kid had seen the flicker of flame from the rifle barrel. Hands reached down for rifles and they expected more bullets to come at them.

'Be off!' a voice yelled from the other side of the open space, up on a darkened slope. 'Don't go near the herd or I'll hit one of you to prove I can.' The Kid's rifle was in his hands. He was almost sure he'd got the speaker located but he heard Knight chuckle, then shout:

'Hold it, Brit. Don't shoot. It's us.'

There was a movement on the other slope in a different place from where the Ysabel Kid expected it. A tall young man came sliding down, rifle in hands. He went to one of the horses and rode across to the others. From the easy way he sat his saddle and the look of his clothes he might have been taken for any cowhand except that as a general rule cowhands did not sport monocles in their right eyes.

'Sorry chaps,' he said cheerfully. 'Didn't recognise you in this light and there were more of you than I expected. Thought it might be some of those bally thugs back again, so I took to my heels and hid away. Jolly bad form and all that rot, but they don't play to the rules themselves.'

Dusty, Mark and the Kid appraised this cool young man. They liked what they saw, for despite his monocle and outlandish way of talking, he was no fool. They'd seen the way he concealed his presence even from the Kid and it raised him in their estimation. In turn Brit was looking them over and with the eye of a man who knew cowhands saw they were more than just three chance hired hands.

'I say, Mr. Knight, you were deuced lucky to be able to take on three more hands at such short notice. I couldn't quite decide how we were going to manage after the others quit,' he paused and looked at Just and Brazos, realising how his words sounded. 'No offence, I knew you and Brazos would stick it out, Just. You're like me, don't have sense enough to get out. There aren't many of us even now.'

'Don't worry none, friend,' Mark answered, looking at the small herd of white-faces. To a man who'd trailed north with a herd of longhorns this would be easy, despite the fact that white-faces did not care to move at night. 'You've got six Texans along with you and everyone knows a Texan is equal to three ordinary men.'

Brit chuckled, 'Modesty is not a virtue amongst you colonials I see.'

'How do you mean, colonials?' Mark asked. 'Didn't you know about the war of seventy-six?'

'My dear chap,' Brit surveyed Mark through his monocle. 'Don't *you* know the world is divided into two parts. Britain and her colonies.'

'What happened, Brit?' Hamilton put in before the usual argument could start. 'We thought you were dead.'

'No such luck, sir. I think I was meant to be and would have been if Lenny hadn't been having a bit of a game. I'd loaned him me monocle to try out. I think the bullet was meant for me.'

'Why?' Dusty asked, leaning forward in his saddle.

'We were both riding bays. I'd been past the place where he was shot twice and nothing happened, so had nearly every man of the crew.'

'That figgers, the try at Just in town ties in with it,' Dusty's voice was low. 'They wanted to get the men who'd stick by KH.'

'Tried for Just, too, did they?' Brit growled. 'Dash it all, we'll have to take stern measures with them. I took after the feller who shot Lenny, he left fast. When I came back Carron was taking the others back to the ranch house. I've buried Lenny. I'll come out tomorrow and put a marker on his grave. Then I hope to get a crack at the blighter who killed him.'

'If that *hombre* took out we'd best move too,' Dusty drawled, looking at Knight. 'He might be back with friends and these white-faces'd spook easy in the dark.'

'Right,' Knight agreed. 'Me'n Mike better take the point, Dusty. We know the range and——' He came to a stop, not knowing how to go on for both Dusty and Mark were known as trail bosses.

'I'm only one of the hands, that was how you took me on, not as trail boss or point rider.'

'You take the swing then,' Knight liked Dusty even more now. He was a natural leader but he did not mind taking orders as well as giving them. 'Head 'em up. Point 'em for the house.'

Before they started the herd moving Just found time to introduce Brit to the three young Texans. He saw the Englishman give Dusty a keen and interested glance and put it down to Brit's having heard of Dusty since he came west. There was no time for more talk for Knight and Hamilton were heading for the herd.

Starting a herd moving was a ticklish business any time and with these sort of cattle at night, even worse. The thing was to get the herd moving under control without stampeding it. The white-faces were a far different proposition from the half wild longhorns which could run like jack-rabbits and fight like lions. The longhorn would, if he could be caught, move as willingly at night as in the daytime. The white-faces, particularly when on a comfortable bed ground would rather not move at all.

With stinging rope ends, shrill yells and charging horses the men got the cattle up and moving. Knight and Hamilton fell in with their horses on either side of the big old bull who'd established himself as the leader. They pointed him towards the KH house and the other cattle moved along after him. On opposite sides of the herd Dusty and Mark moved in about a third of the way along the line, taking the swing positions, then Just and Brit came in behind them as the flank riders while Brazos and the Ysabel Kid brought up the rear. The Kid was for once riding the drag instead of ahead as scout. There was little need of a scout on this short drive and he wanted to be in a position to hear any pursuit should it come. He was wishing he was afork his big white stallion for the horse was trained to warn him of approaching men.

Surrounded by the fast riding men the herd was kept going. Occasionally a steer would break from the line and try to escape, only to be turned back again by a fast riding man on a well-trained horse. Then the sun went right down and darkness blanketed the land. The white-faces tended to bunch up now and keep moving without trying to escape, sticking close to each other for comfort and company.

Handling the herd had its advantages. There was no dust to rise and half-blind the drag riders and the night was cool. Against this was the slow pace they were forced to hold. Knight and Hamilton did not try to force the leader any, for to do so might have turned him baulky and that would have been disastrous in the darkness.

Then the moon came up, full and bright, lighting the range country with a pale glow. The cattle settled down to moving along as a steady herd when they could see where they were going. Apart from the ever present coyotes there was no sound other than the cattle noises, and nothing to make any of the riders suspicious.

Brit caught up with Dusty, his teeth gleamed in the darkness as he asked, 'Are you the Captain Fog who used to ride in the Texas Light Cavalry during the War Between the States?'

'Why sure,' Dusty agreed, wondering where the Englishman had heard of him.

'Good lord, you couldn't have been very old then.'

'I was seventeen when I made Captain, been a Lieutenant for a year before that. How'd you hear about me?'

'My dear man, you're quite famous. Why, the way you handled your troop changed the entire thinking on light cavalry tactics. I was in the 14th Lancers and knew a chappie who was over here as a military observer. Heard him talk about you. He used to get into violent arguments about your tactics with one of the old school.'

Dusty grinned. He'd heard some stiff arguments about his tactics as a light cavalry commander himself. 'Were you in the Army?'

'For a time. It's the thing, you know. Went out to India as a subaltern hoping to have some excitement, but damn if the Regiment wasn't ordered back home just after I arrived. I asked for a transfer to the Bengal Lancers and when I couldn't get it I handed in my papers and came over here to the colonies. Moved West and took on with the KH as a cowhand. Deuced interesting work I find.'

They separated again, both busy with the cattle which were again showing signs of being restless and uneasy. It kept Dusty busy until they reached the lip of the coulee and too late he saw how near they were. It had been his intention to suggest sending the Kid ahead as a scout along the rim of the coulee but he was too late to get permission from either Knight or Hamilton now. In all matters of range work Dusty was scrupulously correct. He was riding with this herd as a hand, and without the permission of the trail boss he could not send the Kid away from the herd.

Standing in his stirrups Dusty studied the range ahead of him. The coulee edges looked clear enough but there were many places where an ambush could be laid and the ambushers remain concealed. He felt uneasy and was about to shout to Knight when he saw he was too late. They were turning the herd down the slope and into the coulee bottom.

Knight moved his horse towards the leading animal while Hamilton pulled his away. The big old bull moved away from the approaching horse and in doing so made for the slope. The rest of the cattle began to close up again, scuttling after the leader and bunching down to less than half the length they'd covered out in the open. The coulee was lit by the moon on the flank where Dusty, Brit and Brazos rode, but Mark and Just were in the deep shadow.

The Ysabel Kid was uneasy. He was alert and his instincts, always more Indian than white, warned him all was not well. He dropped back from his place on the drag, halting the horse and looking all round. There was nothing he could see and yet the feeling was still there. The old Model 66 Winchester slid from the saddleboot into his hands. With his big white stallion he would have been satisfied, for the horse would have warned him of any danger. This was not his old Nigger horse, but was one of the KH remuda, better at cattle work but not so alerted in other and less usual duties.

Knight and Hamilton were now turning the lead animal towards the up-slope again. Hamilton came out of the shadows and into plain view as the two men hazed the big bull towards the up-slope once more.

The Ysabel Kid looked up at the rim they'd just come down. He'd been concentrating on the one they were making for. He gave a yell which was drowned by the noise of the cattle. From above a rifle cracked and men suddenly lined the rim.

CHAPTER SIX

DUSTY TAKES COMMAND

EVEN before the Kid's rifle came up he saw he was too late. Knight went pitching from his saddle. The man who'd shot Jack Knight was in plain view, a big man the Kid would never forget. The man's rifle swung and barked again, even before the other men started shooting, Hamilton arched his back as the lead smashed home and he came down from his horse.

Dusty left his saddle, lead humming over his head even as he fell. Like a true cavalryman he kept the reins of his horse in one hand, the other brought out his Colt. He landed on the ground partly hidden behind his horse and tried to line his gun. All around him the already scared cattle were moving restlessly, snorting and bellowing as the leader stopped. He saw Brit was also off his horse holding it and the horse the murdered man was riding when he left the spread that morning. Brazos was laying on the ground, blood oozing from a hole in his shoulder.

On the other side of the herd Just and Mark could see what was happening, but while in no danger themselves from the men on the rim, they could not get a shot at their attackers, nor could they force their way through the close packed cattle to get out and help their friends.

It was then the Ysabel Kid tried to take a hand, his old yellow boy flowing to his shoulder. He saw a short, slim man in dark clothes appear. The man held something in his right hand, in his left a glowing cigar which he brought down. There was a spluttering scatter of sparks and the man's right hand jerked, throwing the thing down. The Ysabel Kid knew what that thing was. His rifle swung at the man, trying to line on him.

The Kid forgot he was not afork his old Nigger horse. The big white would have stood like a rock even with a fire under him. This cowhorse was not so well trained, and the shooting was making him fiddlefoot nervously. At the crack of the Kid's rifle the horse gave a bounding leap which would have unseated a lesser man.

The roar of an explosion from the centre of the herd made the horse wild with panic. The scene at the bottom of the coulee was like a madhouse. Cattle bellowed in fear, screamed in pain and broke in all directions. The Ysabel Kid saw Mark's horse go down and his Comanche blood erupted. He came off the horse in a leap, letting it tear off in wild stampede. His rifle came up, throwing lead as fast as he could work the lever. One man on the rim. standing next to the one who threw the dynamite into the herd, spun round, clawing at his face and dropped. A second gave a shrill cry and reeled back out of sight. The rest of them turned and backed off out of sight and were gone.

So was the herd.

The white-faces, terrified by the shooting and the explosion were all running, scattering along the coulee in either direction. The Ysabel Kid watched them streaming past him and cursed savagely in three different languages. He lowered the rifle and looked at the writhing, bloody heaps of torn flesh which shortly before were living animals. Over fifteen head of the herd were down, the others would run until they dropped of exhaustion and there was no chance of stopping them.

Just Smith was still on his horse, fighting it for control and knowing the horse would be of no use to him for cattle work while it was spooked. He tried to send the horse across the coulee bottom to where Brit and Dusty were heading for Knight and Hamilton. He twisted round in his saddle and saw Mark's horse was down. The Ysabel Kid was running towards his friend, more expression showing on his face than was usual.

'Mark! You all right?' the Kid yelled.

Slowly Mark forced himself up on his hands and knees, shaking his head. The Kid's arm shot out to help Mark rise and steady him for a moment, then the dazed expression left Mark's eyes.

'I'm all right, Lon. The herd caught most of the blast. Reckon it was part of one of the steers that got my horse. I was already going down when the hoss was hit. Is Dusty all right?'

'Sure. I saw him drop before the shooting. He's with the bosses.'

Mark started across the coulee bottom, his face white under the tan. The Ysabel Kid stayed only long enough to lower his rifle and put the horse out of its misery, then he followed.

Just Smith looked up from Hamilton's side as the others came over. 'He's cashed!'

None of the other men replied. Brit was attending to old Brazos' wound, while Dusty gently pillowed Knight's head on his knees. There was no hope for the rancher, that bullet struck him in the centre of the back and tore right through. It was a miracle he'd lived as long as this.

Knight's eyes opened and looked around. For a moment they did not focus, then they cleared and looked at Mark. 'Is Mike——?'

'Dead, Uncle Jack,' Mark's voice was low and vibrant with anger.

'Dusty—here?'

'Right here.'

'You're foreman now. Take—care—of—the—girls——'

Knight's body gave a convulsive heave, blood rushed from his mouth and then he was still. Gently Dusty lowered the head to the floor and got to his feet. In the moonlight his face looked old and haggard, his clenched fists shook by his sides.

'Why the hell didn't I send the Kid to scout that rim?' he asked, his voice hard, yet he was not speaking to the others. 'God, what a fool I was. I'll never forgive myself for this. I should have known they'd lay for us there. How can I face——'

'Easy, boy,' Mark laid a hand on his friend's shoulder. 'You couldn't know about this.'

'I should have known, or guessed. They know the country and—— Hellfire, Mark, I should have known. I'll never forgive myself——'

Brit came up, looking at Dusty. 'You're not at fault, old boy. It wasn't your place as a hand to send the scout out. I know neither Jack nor Mike would blame you. You don't know this range, you couldn't have known how near we were to this damned place.'

'I agree with Brit.' Just put in. 'Likewise I'm ready to do whatever you want me to.'

For a moment Dusty stood still, his hands clenched, his face drawn in a tight mask. Then the feeling of responsibility came over him again and he took command with the ease of a born leader of men. His first concern was for the wounded.

'How's Brazos?'

'Far as I can tell, not being a surgical Johnny, the bullet went on through without any serious damage or breaking of bone. I've plugged the hole as well as I could. Do anything more I can for him now.'

'No, Just, you tend to it. Mark, I reckon you should take over.'

'I don't,' Mark was adamant. 'Comes cattle work I reckon we both know about as much. Comes fighting you make me look like a yearling. And it's come to fighting right now.'

'When do we take out after them?' the Ysabel Kid's tones were Comanche mean and in the moonlight his face would have passed for one of his grandfather's braves.

'We don't. I'm taking one of these horses, Brit another and you a third. We're headed back to the spread. Someone has to tell the girls. I'd like you along, Brit. I'm not good at words and I reckon you can help me out some. You'll get that old Nigger hoss and head for town as soon as we reach the house, Lon. I want the sheriff telling and the undertaker. I want the sheriff here as soon as he can get. Then you come right straight back to the house. Don't go any other place. Did any of you recognise them?'

'It was Snag Willet used the rifle and killed the bosses,' Brazos answered, biting down the pain of his wounded shoulder. 'And I'd near on swear it was Santone hisself threw the dynamite down.'

'Willet's mine,' Mark said in a soft, mild tone that sounded far more deadly than any amount of wild screamed curses.

'He's yours,' Dusty agreed. 'But right now I want you and Just to stay on here with Brazos. One of you use the hoss and try to collect the herd together again. Brit and me'll be bringing more horses from the remuda and we'll gather the cattle again.'

'I don't want to argue with you, Dusty old chap,' Brit interrupted, 'or go against your orders. But we cut the range very thoroughly to raise those three hundred head. There wasn't another white-face to be found and with around twenty dead we can't produce enough to make up the necessary amount for the banker.'

'All right, thanks, Brit,' Dusty was willing to accept the advice of a man who knew more about local conditions than he himself did. 'We'll tend to the banker when he comes.... Right now we'd best move on out.'

Dusty, Brit and the Kid swung afork their horses and rode up the slope. The sound of the horses faded rapidly into the distance and Mark stood looking down at his uncle's body. For a moment he stood like a statue, then shook his head and walked to where a white-face cow was moaning in agony. He drew his Colt and shot the animal, then walked to the still shape of the horse he'd been riding. Loosening the double girths he used his strength to get the saddle free. His rifle was on top, which was a relief to him. He went on up the slope with the rifle in his hands, looking at the place where the ambushers had hidden. He was in that cold, deadly rage which only an immensely strong, powerful and generally amiable young man could feel. There was a hellish hardness about his face as he went to the bodies of the Kid's victims. The two men were dead, which was as well for them. In his present mood Mark would have shown no mercy to any of the attackers had they fallen into his hands.

Rolling the bodies over with cold, dispassionate hands Mark looked down at them. They were a pair of cheap, hired guns or he missed his guess, the kind who would fight for anyone as long as the pay lasted. He doubted if there would be anything to identify them. Turning, Mark left the two bodies where they lay. He did not intend to waste time burying them; they could lay there and rot for all of him.

Dusty, the Kid and Brit rode for a time without speaking,

each man busy with his own thoughts. Dusty was still bitterly blaming himself for the attack. He should have sent Lon ahead to make a scout. Now through his negligence two men were dead and the herd scattered. For once in his wild, reckless life the Ysabel Kid was finding himself wanting. He'd forgotten one basic fact, he was riding a strange horse, not his big white. That was why the ambush succeeded. Because he forgot all horses were not trained to locate hidden men and give warning of such. Brit was thinking of the two girls, one of them a countrywoman of his. He did not know Gloria and was not sure how either girl would react when told their parents were dead.

Looking at Dusty, Brit was fully aware of the latent danger about the small man. Yet somehow Brit was not really aware Dusty was smaller than he. The young Texan seemed to be the biggest man of them all. Brit had been a soldier and came of a long line of army men, and he knew a born leader when he saw one. It was an aura which set on the shoulders of some men and made others turn to them for leadership in times of danger. Dusty Fog had that aura, and it made him what he was.

'You're not dressed, amigo.'

Brit looked round in surprise at the Ysabel Kid, not quite following the meaning at first. Then he dropped his hand to his gunless side and replied, 'I see what you mean. Got a revolver at the house but I can never seem to hit a deuced thing with it. Now this,' he pulled the Winchester from his saddleboot, 'is the finest rifle I've ever seen.'

It was then the Ysabel Kid saw the rifle was not a yellow boy, but an even better looking weapon. The butt and the frame were made of iron, instead of brass as in the old model the Kid carried. 'That's new, isn't it?'

'The latest model. Uses the new centrefire ammunition,' Brit replied. 'Called the forty-four-forty. Uses a full forty grain powder charge. I bought it as soon as I arrived in New York. Had one of the old models in India. Rajah of one of the small states offered me two elephants, a string of polo ponies and three dancing girls for it. Almost took him up on the offer.'

'Why didn't you?' Dusty asked, more to take his mind off thinking about what he regarded as a failure on his part.

'My dear chap, what would I do with three dancing girls?'

'You should ask your mother that, not us,' the Kid replied, looking at the new model rifle with covetous gaze. The gun, which was to become known as the Model 73, was as much an improvement over the old yellow boy as that trusty rifle had been over previous long guns.

They were coming in sight of the house now, although it was still a fair distance away. Dusty was pale now, his voice shaky. 'I need help, Brit. I've never been so scared in my life.'

'I'll do what I can,' Brit promised. 'This is a bad business, Dusty. Miss Hamilton is only newly arrived from home, I suppose.'

'I've given that some thought, too. It'll not be easy on either of them, will it?'

'It won't, but I'm not unhappy to know you are here. Just, Brazos and I would have stayed on to the last ditch but without more men we wouldn't have much of a chance.'

'Man'd say we don't have much chance right now,' Dusty answered. 'The odds are high against us.'

'I did hear about a fight at some place called the Alamo. You colonial chappies didn't do too badly against the odds there.'

Dusty chuckled. In spite of his anxiety he could appreciate the young Englishman's cool attitude and quiet sense of humour. He'd always thought the English a peculiar, stuffy and humourless people but Brit was far from what he expected. 'We didn't do too badly in seventy-six, either.'

'My dear chap,' Brit eyed Dusty through his monocle in a severe way, copied from his form-master at Eton. 'You were part of us then.'

The Ysabel Kid whistled through his teeth. He was silent and letting the other two talk. Then he spoke, although his words did not appear to have any connection with anything said before, 'Wonder if Cousin Bill's still working on the Baker place, down in Lee County?'

This was over Brit's head, but Dusty knew straight away what the Kid was thinking. It was real smart thinking and opened up a whole lot of possibilities.

'Comes morning I'll ask Mark to go into town and send a

telegraph message off and find out. There's a few other gents I'd like to know about at the same time.'

Brit could not see how this followed on from what they'd been talking about, but he did not ask, for they were nearly to the house now. None of them spoke again as they came to the corral and swung down from the horses. The Kid whistled and like a ghost his big white stallion materialised from out of the night, followed by the paint and the blood-bay.

Removing the saddle from his borrowed horse the Kid changed to his white. His own saddle was headed across the range somewhere but he knew the horse would return with it to the ranch house when the panic died. He pulled the dead cowhand's rifle from the saddleboot and shoved his own Winchester into it, then swung afork the white.

'Lon!' Dusty's voice cut across as the Kid turned his horse to head for town. 'You come straight back here. Not by way of Santone's.'

The Kid's teeth flashed white against the darkness of his face. 'Don't you trust lil ole me?'

'In a word, no. You come right back here.'

The Ysabel Kid gave a mocking laugh and turned his horse, heading for the town at a fast lope. Without the orders just given he would have headed for the Lazy F and settled accounts with Santone or gone under in the attempt. Now he would return here straight after delivering his message and delay his attack. Even as he rode for town he found himself muttering a Comanche Dog Soldier lodge oath that Santone would not be alive by the end of the week, or the Ysabel Kid would be dead.

Brit watched the young man riding away. 'I've never seen a man who looked so dangerous as the Kid. He reminds me of the hillmen on the North-west Frontier of India.'

'Lon's real dangerous all right. More so right now. He's feeling bad about the ambush, like I am. He's the best scout in the west and I don't bar either Cheyenne Bodie or Bronco Layne from the list. He's feeling bad about not seeing the ambush. God help anybody who crosses him right now.'

Dusty stood for a moment looking at the house. Then he shook his head and started forward. Brit followed, watching

Dusty, knowing the Texan would rather be leading a cavalry charge against a regiment than facing the task of telling the two girls the news.

They stepped on to the porch and Dusty was about to knock when Brit reached for a small knob set at the side and pulled it. From inside the house somewhere a bell jangled loud in the stillness. Brit's face held a smile like the grin on a skull as he turned to Dusty. 'I fitted that up for the bosses. Jack was amused by it, said it gave the place a bit of real tone. All we needed was a butler to answer it.'

From up above a window was lifted and the sound of a Winchester rifle being cocked came to their ears. Then a sleepy voice asked, 'Who is it?'

'Me'n Brit, Miss Gloria,' Dusty replied, stepping back out where the girl could see him.

'I'll be down in a minute.'

Gloria's head and rifle disappeared again and the window closed down. Dusty returned to the porch and stood by Brit, conscious the young Englishman's breathing was heavy and knowing Brit was not relishing this. They stood in silence, then through the transom of the door saw a glow of light and heard footsteps.

The door opened and a lantern bathed them in light. Gloria stood in the hall, the lantern in her hands throwing its light over her. Brit never forgot his first view of the girl, her hair rumpled and untidy, her pretty face flushed and sleepy eyed, her nightgown covered by a long housecoat and her feet bare. Behind her, dressed in the same way, face paler yet still schooled and aloof stood Rene.

'Hey Dusty,' Gloria greeted, smiling. 'You boys come ahead of the others?'

'Mind if we come in, Miss Gloria?'

'Come ahead,' Gloria replied, her smile fading as she saw the expression on Dusty's face and knew something very bad was wrong. Her instincts almost made her clairvoyant and she licked her lips. 'What is it, Dusty?'

Watching the two men walk by her Gloria was struck by the serious looks on their faces. She hardly noticed the monocle which looked so incongruous in Brit's eye, hardly even noticed him at all, her full attention being on the young Texan. For a moment Dusty's eyes met hers, then looked away but in that brief exchange of glances Gloria was almost sure she knew what was wrong. Her legs felt weak and for once she could hardly think, let alone speak.

'What is it, Dusty?' Rene came forward. She too could see the worry on the face of the young Texan and knew that something very serious had happened.

Dusty took a deep breath and tried to think of a suitable reply. In the war he'd twice been in the same sort of position, telling of the death of a loved one. He'd not liked the task then and he liked it far less now. He looked at Brit and the young Englishman suggested they went into the sitting-room. Gloria led the way, lighting the big lamp on the table with hands that shook.

'Dusty,' her voice was urgent. 'What is it?'

Dusty tried to avoid her eyes, looking round the large room. It was a comfortable looking room, with a polish-topped table and half a dozen straight backed chairs in the centre. Other deep, comfortable looking armchairs were in the corners. The walls on three sides were decorated with painting. The fourth had a large, open fireplace with a cupboard on either side of it. Over the fireplace was hung a pair of crossed Comanche war lances, a buffalo shield, a war bow and a quiver of arrows. At last he looked back at the girls who took a deep breath.

'Is it the herd?' Rene asked, her voice even.

'It's pappy, isn't it?' Gloria spoke in a strangled voice.

This was the moment Dusty feared. The moment when he must tell the girls the truth. 'Yes, your pappy and Mr. Hamilton.'

Gloria stood rigid, her face losing all its colour. 'Are they——?'

'Yes, both of them. Killed without a chance.'

CHAPTER SEVEN

THE NOTE FALLS DUE

Gloria's breath came out in a quick gasp. She stood for an instant without a move. Then with a cry she twisted round and into Rene's arms. The blonde girl's face was even paler, but she held Gloria to her and soothed the sobbing girl as if she was handling a baby. It took several minutes before Gloria could get control of her nerves again. Her eyelids were red and swollen as she turned a tear-stained face to Dusty but her voice was steady and without trace of hysteria.

'How did it happen, Dusty?'

'We were bushwhacked out at the coulee. They had us whipsawed, under their guns.' He braced himself and went on. 'It was all my fault. I——'

'No Dusty!' Gloria took his hands in hers. 'Pappy was bossing the drive, you were riding as a hand. You aren't at fault. What happened?'

'One of the men shot down your father and Mr. Hamilton. The others were shooting at us, then Santone threw dynamite into the herd. The Kid got two of them but the rest pulled out.'

Rene looked at the young man. Gloria had told her much about this small, insignificant-looking young man; things she could hardly believe, even though she knew Gloria would not be lying. She also knew he was blaming himself bitterly for the ambush and his failure to prevent it. She came alongside Gloria, her face still schooled as she fought to hold down her grief. Placing her arm round Gloria's shoulders she looked straight at Dusty.

'We do not blame you, Captain Fog. Nor do we think you

failed us in any way. Are the others all right?'

'Brazos took lead in the shoulder and we lost a few horses but the herd's scattered and we won't be able to gather it again in time. Just and Mark stayed out there with——' He paused, then went on. 'Brit'll be taking fresh horses and a wagon out there.'

'Where's the Kid?' There was a sudden suspicion in Gloria's voice, for she knew much about the way of Loncey Dalton Ysabel.

'I sent him to town to notify the sheriff, not that it'll do us any good. Like I said, the man who led the raid and threw the dynamite was Santone and the sheriff won't move against him. Comes morning Mark, Lon and I'll make our own move against Santone.'

'No you won't,' Gloria snapped. 'They'll be expecting you and we need every man here tomorrow. Pappy would want you to take over as foreman, Dusty. So do we. I don't want the boys riding out tomorrow.'

'I'll see to it,' Dusty promised, knowing all the men would be needed to attend to the burying of the two ranchers.

For the first time Rene spoke an order. 'Leave it to the law, Dusty.'

'The law in Azul Rio belongs to Lanton, I'm afraid, Miss Hamilton,' Brit put in, his accent matching her own in its cultured sound. 'We can expect no help from him. The only law for KH is what we make ourselves.'

'This is Brit, Miss Gloria, Miss Hamilton,' Dusty remembered the girls did not know the other man.

'Charmed,' Brit said, putting more than just formal feeling into the word as he took Gloria's offered hand, then turned with a smile to Rene. 'I think we've met before.'

Rene stared at Brit, her face showing some emotion for once, surprise and interest crossing the carefully schooled features. 'Good heavens, you're the Ear——!'

'Here I am known as Brit, Miss Knight, and I would prefer to remain that way, please.'

She stopped at the gentle interruption, hardly knowing how to carry on. Gloria could see her friend's difficulty. 'I'll make you a cup of coffee before you go back to the herd,' she said. 'Come and help me, Rene.'

'Of course.' Rene was only too pleased to have something

to do, even if it was only helping to make a cup of coffee. At the door she stopped and looked back. 'You said the Kid has gone to town. Was that wise, Dusty. He might meet some of the men who——'

'He might at that and it will be real dangerous. *For them.* He's on his old Nigger horse now and that white can smell a hidden man like a redbone hound hitting a coon line. If they try to ambush the Kid I pity them. I'd back him in the dark against the best Lanton's got and then some.'

While waiting for the coffee Dusty and Brit went out to harness a team to the chuckwagon in the barn, and catch fresh horses for the other members of the crew. They returned and drank the coffee, hardly tasting it and not talking. At last Dusty rose and went to the girls, 'We'll be back as soon as we can. You'd better stay in one room, Miss Rene.' She looked at him, face strained and holding back tears. 'Sometimes it helps to cry.'

The following morning the men of the ranch crew sat around the table moodily eating their breakfast. Old Brazos was leaning back in a chair, his arm in a sling and bandages showing under his shirt collar. Every one of them was unshaven, faces lined with lack of sleep and worry. It was the Ysabel Kid, looking mean and more Comanche than ever, who put the question on all their minds.

'When do we ride?'

'Not until Gloria says so and it won't be yet,' Dusty answered. 'So you just sit and simmer down.'

He could read mutiny in every face as the others looked at him and knew they would be hard to hold. Then the door of the room opened and Brit rose to his feet, followed by the others as the girls came in. They both wore simple black dresses and their faces bore mute testimony to the grief they were feeling. Yet both were composed as they took the seats offered to them by the men. Rene looked at the circle of faces around the table and stood up again.

'I would like to thank all of you for what you've done for us.'

'Thanks aren't necessary, Miss Hamilton. We regret it was not enough,' Brit answered for the others, removing his monocle and polishing it, conscious that Gloria was looking at him with considerable interest. 'I think I can say for all of us that we are at your service for as long as you wish.'

'Which won't be long,' Gloria put in. 'You're forgetting the bank note falls due today. The banker'll be coming out here at nine o'clock and he'll want either the herd or the money.'

'Hell, I could let you have the money but I'm short right now,' Mark put in. 'But you know pappy'll send it along to you as soon as he hears.'

'I know that, but the banker works for Lanton. He's not going to wait, he'll be coming to foreclose, not to get paid.'

Mark's fist lifted and crashed down on to the table hard enough to make the plates and cups leap. 'He'll wait or I'll make him wish he'd never been born.'

'Which same won't help none,' Dusty remarked, knowing Mark was quite capable of carrying out his threat. 'They've got the law on their side and I don't just mean that fat nogood in town there. We could handle him but we can't fight Uncle Sam.'

'Dusty's right on that,' Gloria agreed. 'Besides Uncle Mike and pappy took the money in good faith and no matter who the banker is we're paying him back the same way.'

'Hell, this whole damned business was rigged to get the KH,' the Kid growled. 'I say to hell with the banker and let's take Lanton right now.'

There was a rumble of agreement from Mark, Brazos and Just at this. Gloria looked around the table, knowing the men were willing to fight and die for her. She was about to speak when Brit coughed and removed his monocle once more.

'Ladies, your fathers hired me in the fond belief they were helping a down and out rip. I may be a rip but I am not quite down and far from out. Came out here to find a bit of excitement. The old world's a bit played out for that sort of thing, don't you know. Wanted to learn the cattle business with the view to taking a suitable place. Anyway, I appear to be waffling on somewhat but what I want to say is, if you'll accept it in no sense as being charity, I am willing to loan you the money. Right now.' He reached into his shirt and took out a thick, pigskin wallet with a gaudy coloured seal engraved on it. 'There's three thousand dollars there for the banker and I have more if it is needed.'

Rene took the wallet, feeling the weight of it and looking at Gloria. For once in her life the little redhead could not think of any suitable words for an occasion. It was left to Rene to reply.

'Thank you, my lo——'

'Brit!' he gently reminded her.

'Thank you, Brit. I have enough money to cover the loan but it hasn't been transferred over here yet. I thank you for both Gloria and myself.'

'Now hold hard for a minute,' Gloria snapped. 'This is a partnership and you aren't going to pay it all back. Brit, the ranch is the security on your loan.'

'My dear young lady,' Brit eyed Gloria severely, screwing his monocle into his eye again. 'I require no security other than your guarantee of permanent employment on the KH.'

Gloria had to smile, despite her misery. The young Englishman, with his strange accent and his monocle was something she'd never met before. He was so cool and calm about everything and she suspected the monocle was no more than an affectation. 'One more useless loafer round the place won't make any difference,' she answered. 'Now you bunch get some sleep.'

'Later,' Dusty came to his feet, once more in command. 'Just, you and Mark tend to that chore I gave you. Brit, you and the Kid look to the remuda. Brazos, you're riding the wagon for a spell, get to bed and from under foot. Gloria, I reckon you and Rene got some work to do so don't sit around the fire all the morning.'

Gloria came to her feet. She knew Dusty was giving her and Rene work to stop them brooding. Coming to a military brace she raised her hand in a salute. 'Yes, sir, Cap'n Fog, sir. Right away, come on Rene. That's how you tell a ranch foreman. He can't rest and doesn't want anybody else to get any either.'

'The banker's coming, Dusty.'

The Ysabel Kid came into the barn where Dusty was watching the Azul Rio undertaker preparing the bodies for burial. Dusty turned and went to the door, looking out. 'Stay on here, Lon,' he ordered. 'Mark, come along and see what comes out.'

Banker Ames drove his buggy in front of the KH house and halted. He was a tall, florid. well-dressed man with the smooth skin of an Eastern dude. His clothes were faultlessly cut and he wore them well, his entire appearance being one of well-being and self-assurance. He was vaguely worried as he climbed down from the buggy, for he'd heard of the killing of the two ranchers. The rumour he'd been given was the rest of the KH crew were either dead, departed, or so badly wounded they would be able to do nothing either in defence or offence. He felt the bulge of the title deeds in his inside coat pocket. There was little need to have brought the deeds along except as a matter of form. He was coming to take the ranch, not hand over the deeds.

Looking at the two girls standing side by side on the porch he was struck by the pallid beauty of the former and the forlorn dejection of the smaller. He could read the grief in their faces as he came nearer. The blonde's expression told him nothing but the other looked as if the world was coming to an end. It was the look of a woman who sees her home gone from her.

'I must express my deepest regret at your bereavement, ladies,' he said, his voice oily and ingratiating. 'I was deeply shocked to think such a thing could happen in the Azul Rio.'

'It was one of your respected ranchers did the killing.'

Ames turned to see who was speaking, for the voice came from the side of the house and was definitely masculine. Two hard-faced young Texas men came into view, their hardness not helped by the fact that neither of them had shaved. They advanced, looking as friendly and amiable as a couple of razorback hogs stropping up against a fence ready to take on all hands. The banker licked his lips, looking down at their hands as they stood there with thumbs hooked into gunbelts. There was a mistake somewhere, neither of this pair were wounded or incapacitated in any way.

'Much as I regret the necessity,' Ames decided that nothing would be gained by answering the young men and turned his attention back to the two girls on the porch, 'I have to ask you for the payment of this note. Either three thousand dollars or three hundred head of white-face cattle.'

'Today?' Gloria sounded pathetic.

'I'm afraid so. The bank must conduct all its business on time.'

'Man, I bet you have a whingding when you're foreclosing on some poor ole widderwoman,' Mark growled.

'Really, Miss Knight,' Ames turned his face to the girl. 'This is most uncalled for. Tell your hired men to keep out of my business.'

'I wouldn't be in it for the world,' Dusty drawled. 'I'm not part rattler.'

'Dusty, please,' Gloria cut in. She was playing a part and having enough trouble holding the pose without this added distraction. 'This is my foreman, Captain Dusty Fog, and my cousin, Mark Counter.'

'Tell Lanton when you see him,' Mark said, moving to stand alongside Gloria. 'It'll make his day.'

The banker gulped. There would be some difficulty in evicting the two girls if they could not pay. Public opinion would be against the move and the county sheriff was not the sort who could handle either of these hard-eyed young Texas men.

'About the money?'

'What do you aim to do if we tell you to go straight to hell and fry there?' Mark inquired.

'I will be compelled to call in the Federal law,' Ames replied, knowing the threat of local law would hardly deter or frighten Dusty Fog and Mark Counter. 'But surely there will be no need for that, ladies. You are too sensible to allow such folly, it will only make bad trouble.'

'Come into the office then,' Gloria suggested.

Rene was watching all this and thinking what a marvellous actress Gloria would have made. In fact, if Rene did not know of the wallet in Gloria's frock pocket she would have been sure her little friend was not able to pay off the note. In spite of her grief Rene was hard put to hold down laughter at the salty comments Dusty and Mark were making on the subject of bankers.

Gloria led them into the office, the small room facing the sitting-room across the hall. At the open-fronted bureau

Brit was lounged in a chair. He turned round to look as the banker followed the girls in, then swung back to the business of lounging once more. Brit bent forward to hide his face, for he too was impressed by Gloria's acting prowess. He too might have been fooled by her dejected look.

'Please, can't we have more time to pay?' Gloria asked in a tone that would have made a Philadelphia lawyer's heart melt.

'I'm afraid not. I must have the note settled today or——'

'Lanton might not like it,' Dusty finished for Ames.

'That's right, I mean—— Mr. Lanton does not know a thing about this transaction. This is all most unsatisfactory, Miss Knight. I must have the settlement now.'

'Deuced impatient chap, what?' Brit drawled languidly, then turned as if to study the banker for the first time. 'I say, who brought that bally dead fish in here—— Oh, I am sorry, old chappie. Honest mistake and all that sort of rot. The similarity is amazing.'

Ames was almost grinding his teeth in rage. He felt so impotent at the way these men treated him. The monocled eye was cold and dispassionate as it looked at him and as disconcerting as the cold watchful gaze of the two Texas men.

It was then Gloria decided she must cut in and spoil the boys' fun. She could not hold her pose much longer, so taking out the wallet she held it forward. Ames stared down at the pigskin wallet, his hand going out hesitantly, then backing again as if he was afraid it would bite him, Gloria let the wallet fall to the desk top by Brit's hand but Ames still did not attempt to take it.

'Pick it up, dear fellow,' Brit said cheerily. 'It's harmless although a touch gaudy. Had it made in Darjeeling and the cobbler johnny went and decorated it at the same time.'

Hesitantly Ames took up the wallet, opened it and pulled out a sheaf of hundred dollar bills. He stared down at the bills for a moment, then licking his lips started to count them. It took him time for his hands did not want to obey his brain. He hoped to find the money short and was disappointed when he reached the thirtieth bill. Looking like a sick puppy he faced Gloria and Rene who were standing side by side. It was then he realised the small girl had been acting all the time.

'It appears to be all there,' he said, and there was a tremor in his voice.

'You sound disappointed,' Rene remarked.

'Certainly not, Miss Hamilton. I'm always delighted when business is transacted on time. But,' he patted the side of his coat and a sickly smile came to his face, 'I would appear to have left the deeds at the bank.'

'Awkward,' Dusty growled.

'Deuced awkward,' Brit agreed, then his face brightened with inspiration. 'I say, we can let Dusty and Mark take the money to the bank for you along with a note in your hand asking for the deeds. You can stay on here until they get back. It'll be quicker and safer for them than you.'

That did not appeal to Ames, who knew he'd be in bad trouble when the two Texans came back with the news that he was carrying the deeds with him. He reached into the inside pocket and with what he hoped to be well simulated surprise, took out the thick envelope containing the deeds. Forcing a laugh he held them out towards Gloria.

'I'm sorry, they were in my pocket. I thought they were the papers for another deal.'

Brit took the deeds before Gloria could reach them. He looked up at the girl, 'May I?'

'Be my guest,' Gloria replied, smiling. She was beginning to feel even more friendly to this strange talking young man.

'Learned something of the law at Sandhurst,' Brit told the others as he ran through the deeds with a professional gaze. 'Took the liberty of making out a formal receipt. I know you won't mind signing it.'

Ames sank into the chair Brit vacated, taking out his billfold and putting the money into it. He noticed the Texans watching him and wondered if they knew he was carrying a gun. Both Dusty and Mark knew, they'd seen the telltale bulge for they were long used to looking for hidden weapons. They were not surprised to see the banker was armed.

Reaching for the pen which lay on the desk, Ames took the receipt and read it through. The Englishman might talk strangely but he knew his law, for there was no legal loophole left in that receipt. There was one course open to Ames.

'Funny thing about signatures, Dusty,' Brit was saying even as the idea came to Ames. 'Chappie always does them the same way. Take this one here on the deed, I would wager the banker johnny does the one of the receipt exactly the same.'

Ames signed his name at the bottom of the receipt and made sure he used his correct signature. He knew that any deviation from that signature would meet with dire suspicion and painful retaliation. His idea of, at a later date, making a claim that his signature was forged had faded and gone. However, there was one more hole card left to him.

Brit took a sheet of paper from his pocket, glanced at the column of numbers on it, then started to screw it up, saying, 'I shouldn't need this list of the serial numbers of those notes any more.' Stopping, Brit killed Ames' relief unborn. 'Better keep it though. This chappie here just might get robbed on his way back to town and our having the numbers would help the Pinkertons no end.'

Taking up his hat Ames looked at the sheet of paper. 'Perhaps I'd better take the list with me.'

'That would be foolish. If you were robbed they'd take the list with them, wouldn't they? This way *we* know it is safe.'

The banker could see he was beaten now. His last hope would have been to pretend he'd been robbed, given the description of two of the KH men as the robbers. With KH holding the numbers he could not take that chance. He knew the Pinkerton Agency as being a very efficient organisation who never gave up a trail once they were on it. The only way to take care of the money would be to burn it, for the Pinkertons would have the numbers and even after years might find the bills if they were kept and put back into circulation.

There remained only one thing to do now. Admit the ranch was lost to the Syndicate for the time being, Lanton would not like that but there was nothing more he could do. He wished Gloria and Rene goodbye and walked out of the room, ignoring the men.

Rene watched the man walking towards his buggy and shook her head. 'I still don't know why you wanted us to act the way we did, Dusty. You made a bad enemy in him.'

'I never had me a good one yet,' Mark pointed out.

'Or me,' Dusty agreed. 'We played it this way to find out where the banker stood. He might be a conscientious man who wanted to handle his business on time, come what may. Or he might be working for Lanton, which we've proved he is.'

'We surely did,' Mark whooped enthusiastically. 'Redtop, you should have been an actress. You'd make them all look like yearling stock. I like to died the way you acted.'

Brit chuckled. 'May I say that I would pay good money to see you act, Miss Knight.'

She turned and looked at Brit. 'Listen, you glass-eyed whatever you won't let Rene tell us you are. You call me Miss Knight just once more and I'll whup you so fast you'll think the hawgs have jumped you.'

Rene's face turned scarlet. She stared first at Gloria then at the smiling young Englishman. Before the laughing Brit could open his mouth to say anything Rene burst out:

'Gloria, you don't know who you're talking to. This is the Earl of Hawksden.'

CHAPTER EIGHT

RENE CALLS WAR

GLORIA and the others looked at the monocled Englishman. In the Eastern school Gloria got to know the various grades of European nobility and knew exactly what an Earl was. Her face turned red and she gulped, then said, 'I—— I——'

'And as you just now said. Gloria,' Brit interrupted, smiling. 'If you call me anything but Brit I'll take rather severe steps myself.'

Dusty laughed. He knew the grades as well as Gloria but did not mean to allow it to alter his opinion of Brit as a man and a friend. 'Reckon Brit's good enough for me and the boys. We wouldn't remember the rest of it anyways. Where did you and Rene meet?'

'Hunting in Leicestershire,' Rene answered. 'Before the Ear—Brit went to India.'

The Ysabel Kid came into the room, jerking his head towards the door. 'Folks coming, Dusty. Looks like that sheriff and some more along of a buggy. You'd best come on out.'

They all left the office and went on to the porch. The approaching party were coming through the ford. The sheriff rode alongside the buggy, three men wearing stars fanning out around him. Behind the buggy came a tall man riding easily afork a big bay horse. He wore the clothes of a rancher, a low-tied Colt 1860 Army revolver at his side, his face leathery and tanned by the elements. The buggy was driven by a big, fat man; a pretty, dark-haired Mexican girl by his side.

'Who are they, Brit?'

'Lynch, you know him. Three deputies, no accounts all of

them. The chappie at the back is Painthoss. The young lady Miss Estradre.'

'And the other?'

'Lanton!'

'Lanton?' The word came out as a Comanche grunt from the Ysabel Kid, his right hand twisting back around the butt of his old gun.

'Easy, Lon,' Dusty ordered.

Lanton was a big man, as tall as Mark Counter and far heavier from the look of him. He was fat, very fat, his neck appearing to rise the same size as his head. Dressed in sober black Eastern clothes, with a gold watch chain across his vest and a gold signet ring as his only decorations. He was not happy fat, his eyes were small and piggy, his face brutish and his black hair slicked back with bayrum and parted in the centre.

By his side Juanita Estradre sat ramrod straight, her face showing grief, for she'd been very fond of the Knights and felt the death of Jack Knight deeply. In her sober black dress she looked a pathetic sight on the seat of the buggy.

Lanton brought his buggy to a halt in front of the ranch and glanced at Dusty, then snapped, 'Here you! My man! Hold the team while I get down.'

'Go right to hell and fry there,' was the soft drawled reply.

One of the deputies sent his horse forward. 'You do what Mr. Lanton tells you.'

Dusty swung forward off the porch, his face expressionless. He went forward as if to obey. Then as he came level with the deputy his hands shot out, gripped the man's boot and heaved. The deputy yelled as he was pitched out of the saddle. One of the other deputies dropped his hand towards the butt of his gun. Dusty came round, his left hand leaping across his body and bringing out his Colt, the hammer earing back as it lined.

'What I said still goes,' Dusty told Lanton and holstered his gun once more. The deputies both held their hands clear of their guns and the man on the ground lay gasping for breath, the wind knocked out of him by the fall.

Lynch snapped an order and one of the deputies swung down from his saddle to hold the heads of the buggy team.

The man Dusty had thrown from his horse got up but he kept his hands away from his guns. He knew the man he'd spoken to now and knew Dusty Fog could copper any bet he made.

Lanton climbed laboriously from the buggy and held his hand to the Mexican girl but she ignored it and climbed out the other side. Then Lanton turned and for the first time saw Rene Hamilton. His piggy eyes glinted as he looked at the pale, beautiful face. Here was a woman in a thousand, a proud and haughty beauty with grace and poise. She would be a fitting wife for any man. He was about to move towards Rene when he saw the ranch crew converging on him. This was puzzling for his partner, Santone, swore almost every man was badly wounded if not dead.

Juanita went towards Gloria, her face working nervously. 'I am sorry this happened, Gloria. I would not have had it for the world.'

Gloria looked up sharply. They'd never called each other by their correct names but were always Neety and Rojo. Setting her face hard Gloria snapped, 'It was one of your partners who did it. How did you come to tie in with this bunch?'

Juanita was about to speak when Lanton came alongside her. Her face went hard and she took a pace back. 'That is my business.'

Angrily Gloria turned away, not seeing the deep hurt in Juanita's eyes. Lanton stopped at the foot of the porch and looked first at Dusty, then at the girls.

'That was hardly the thing for a hired man to do to a duly appointed officer of the law,' he said, his voice deep and husky.

'On my spread my foreman handles any cheap hired gun any way he wants,' Gloria turned and snapped back.

'Your ranch?' Lanton frowned. 'I thought you had to meet a note to the bank today.'

'We met it, got it paid, receipt signed and deeds locked safe away,' she replied, her voice not hiding the dislike she felt for the man. 'Didn't your banker tell you all about it?'

'My banker?' Lanton looked puzzled. 'You mean Mr.

Ames. We passed him on the trail but he did not stop. May I offer my condolences, Miss Hamilton?'

'How'd you know who Rene was?' Gloria asked before her friend could answer. 'We never said who she was in town.'

'Happen Carron told him,' Dusty suggested and could see he'd guessed correctly.

'Carron?' Lanton was a card player and schooled his features fast. He was revising his views of this small, insignificant looking young man. 'Who might Carron be?'

'A yeller rat the bosses fired. I figured he'd likely head back to his hole as fast as he could go. The same rat who ran to Santone and set us up for the kill.'

'That's a dangerous accusation, young man. Can you prove it?' Lanton hid his surprise at the way Dusty called everything right.

'When I need to I'll prove it.'

The sheriff was watching all this and not knowing what to do, said: 'All right, let's get this inquest started. Let's go——'

'Round here folks take off their hats, they ask, not tell Cousin Gloria when they want something doing. You, being folks, had better try again. Just for me.'

Lynch looked at Mark Counter's hard face and gulped down something, he removed his hat and turned to Gloria. 'Can we start, please, Miss Knight.'

'Sure. Go down to the barn, the undertaker's there,' Gloria held her voice firm. Brit came alongside her, taking her arm gently and escorting her from the porch.

Lanton watched the hard-faced young men who stood around. Though a dude, he'd seen enough of gunmen to know they were as handy looking a bunch as he'd ever seen. One thing he knew for sure was he would need all his men and more to handle them. He'd been expecting to find a pair of grief stricken girls to whom he could magnanimously offer to let stay on at the ranch for a few days. Instead he found them still the owners and backed by a tough bunch of cowhands. He stared at Rene again and would have made an attempt to get near her but his way was blocked by Just Smith, who moved in and took Rene's arm.

For an instant red rage filled Lanton, his hand slipped

under his coat and to the butt of the Webley Bulldog revolver in his shoulder clip. He chanced to glance towards the porch and what he saw brought his hand clear. Lounging on the porch, the Ysabel Kid's hand was still twisted back around the butt of his old Dragoon gun. Lanton had been very close to death at that moment.

'Don't keep the sheriff waiting, fat man,' the Kid growled deep and mean. 'If you weren't his boss he wouldn't like it.'

At the door of the barn the sheriff gulped, remembering something of the procedure for such things. 'You men shouldn't be wearing them guns.'

'I don't reckon we should at that,' Dusty agreed. 'But when I'm near a skunk I like to keep a jar of perfume handy.'

Lynch took the point and did not press the matter any further. He went into the barn followed by his men, the Texans followed them in, fanning along the wall behind Gloria and Rene.

Lanton and the Ysabel Kid were the last in, after Painthoss escorted Juanita inside. The fat man started towards Rene but Just Smith blocked his way. 'Stay on your own side, rangehawg,' he ordered.

For a moment the fat man looked as if he might either say or do something rash but he turned and walked back to stand by the sheriff. Juanita started to say something in Spanish but Lanton stopped her. 'We don't talk anything but English now, do we, dear?'

'I forgot,' Juanita looked straight at the Ysabel Kid. 'Mr. Lanton does not wish me to speak any of my languages, Spanish, French, Yaqui.'

The Kid caught the glance and made an unobtrusive sign. The girl's nod was almost imperceptible and she moved back, away from the others. Her hands started to move and the Kid watched, reading the hardest of all the Indian hand languages, Yaqui sign talk. None of the others gave the girl any attention and would have been hard put to make anything of the signs, for the Yaqui sign was the most difficult of all the tribal talk.

'How did it happen?' the sheriff asked, glancing at the town undertaker.

'Don't you know already?' Dusty inquired.

'I'll tell you how it happened,' Mark went on, his voice deep and vibrant. 'We were bringing a herd back to the ranch house to pay your friend the banker. As we came through the coulee they hit us. Santone threw dynamite into the herd and Snag Willet shot down Uncle Jack and Mike Hamilton in cold blood.'

'How come the bosses of the spread were riding at the point of the herd?' the sheriff asked, then realised he'd made a slip.

'Nobody said they were at the point. Nobody here that is,' Dusty replied. 'Where else would the boss be except at the point, unless he was a fat dude who hired everything done for him.'

Lanton snorted angrily but before he could speak was stopped. Mark Counter pointed to the coffins. 'There lies a pair of good men. Jack Knight and my father were like brothers. Last night he was murdered without a chance of fighting back. You can tell Santone and Snag Willet I'm shooting on sight.'

'You sure it was Santone and Willet done it, friend?' Painthoss spoke for the first time.

'Brazos recognised him, so did Brit and Just.'

'The law will handle this matter, cowboy,' Lanton put in, watching the Ysabel Kid, who now stood alongside Mark. 'I'm afraid you're wrong in blaming my partner and Willet. Mr. Santone was with me at the ranch all last night. Miss Estradre can verify it. Willet was with the hands in the bunkhouse playing cards.'

'Mister,' Dusty's voice was flat and even. 'You're a liar.'

Lanton looked at the small Texan, face working angrily. He knew that in the west no man called another a liar in that tone unless full willing to back up the words with a smoking Colt gun. Lanton would lose face in the eyes of Painthoss by ignoring the remark. He also knew any attempt to take exception with a gun would be a failure from the start.

'As I said, Miss Estradre can verify my words. Is that not so, my dear Juanita?'

Juanita's face was showing a rapid play of emotions but she nodded in agreement. 'It is as Mr. Lanton says.'

Swinging back to face Dusty, Lanton's triumphant expression died an uneasy death before those level, cold grey eyes. 'Does that satisfy you?'

'No, it don't.'

'I will take my oath it is true,' Lanton snarled, he'd never been so completely faced down and humiliated by another man. That it should be happening in front of that beautiful English girl made it far worse. He went on without thinking of the consequences. 'You've come here and there has been one killing after another. Now you start accusing my partner of this heinous crime. How do we know you didn't kill Knight and Hamilton, then steal the herd yourselves?'

There was a sudden hush in the room. The sheriff's face went pale, his men moved towards each other. Gloria and Rene both started to snap out angry denials, then Mark gave a yell of 'Dusty, no!' and moved fast, thrusting the Kid aside hard even as the bowie knife was coming out, shooting his other arm out at Dusty.

Mark was almost too late. He'd seen the anger in Dusty's eyes and the way Dusty's fist folded. The fist was folded normally except that the first finger stuck ahead of the rest in the deadly forefinger fist of Karate, that deadly Japanese fighting art Tommy Okasi taught the smallest of the Hardin, Fog and Blaze clan. The fist was shooting out for the philtrum, that collection of nerve centres under the nose. A blow struck there with the forefinger fist could kill if landed at full strength and that was how Dusty was striking now. Mark only just deflected the fist a fraction, but it was enough. Lanton's head snapped back under the savage and painful impact of the blow but it missed the vital spot. The big man staggered and crashed to the floor.

Snarling in fury Lanton's hand lashed up and across, under his coat. It was a fast move, very fast considering his bulk. The gun was sliding out before Dusty even started his draw. Then Dusty's hands moved, crossing in a flickering blur of movement. The matched guns were out and flame tore from the four and three-quarter inch blued barrels, the two shots so close together they sounded as one. The short barrelled gun was torn from Lanton's hand by the bullet from the right-hand Colt, the left tore a vicious shallow groove across the man's fat cheek and nicked the lobe of his ear. Smoke curled lazily up from the muzzles of Dusty Fog's guns as he looked at the other men.

Lynch and his deputies stood immobile, staring at the men facing them. The Kid was on one knee, his bowie knife still in his hand. Just's right hand was resting on the butt of his gun ready to swivel back the holster and take cards.

Lanton sat up, holding his cheek with his left hand, the right hand numb and useless to him. His piggy eyes glowed hatred and he snarled, 'You shot at a man who was down.'

'Had you been stood I'd have killed you.'

Painthoss stood clear of the other Syndicate men, looking at Dusty Fog. In his time the big rancher had seen the best in action and knew that here was the master of them all. There was no boasting in those simple words. Dusty Fog called his shots the way they went. If Lanton had been on his feet Dusty would have killed him. At first Painthoss, hearing of Slinger's death, thought the young Texan was lucky. Now he knew different, Slinger was not fast enough.

Lanton forced his fat body up, his face twisted in almost maniacal rage. 'Sheriff, arrest that man. He tried to kill me.'

Lynch gulped and took a pace backwards, nearer to his men. That order was the most scaring thing he'd ever heard. To try and arrest Dusty Fog right now would be just the same as walking into a Chicago slaughter-house, passing the pole-axe man and saying hit me. It would be certain death. True, Dusty Fog's guns were back in their holsters again but that meant nothing, for they could be drawn again with that same speed.

Backing the sheriff were three men, all paid for their fighting skill. They might risk stacking up against a man like Dusty Fog if he was alone. But he was not alone. He was backed by his two friends, Mark Counter and the Ysabel Kid, either of whom would give pause to a better man than Lynch or his deputies. They were also backed by Just Smith who was almost in their class with a gun himself. Even the young Englishman was a hard hand willing to take cards even though he did not wear a gun.

It was too much for Lynch. He knew his men would not back him up and that Lanton was unarmed, the short barrelled gun laying broken on the floor. He knew Painthoss would not side with him. The rancher was far from a willing member of the Syndicate and would be only too pleased to see the leading light of it go under before the guns of the Texans.

Glancing back Lynch knew the truth. His men were scared, and they would not back him up. He licked his lips nervously, his next move being either the end of his life or his finish as Lanton's sheriff. His fingers worked spasmodically, his scared eyes going to Painthoss for support and finding only mocking contempt. Lanton was watching Lynch and waiting for something to happen. It was a dangerous situation, like sitting amongst scattered, fused sticks of dynamite and tossing burning matches around.

Then Rene moved, leaving Gloria's side and going between the two opposing factions, her eyes blazing with fury.

'Dusty, get back to the wall. Lon, put that knife away!' she hissed, her voice vibrant. The orders were obeyed without a question and the KH men drew back, leaving her to turn on Lanton. She ignored the sheriff as if he was something beneath her feet. 'And you, *sir*,' never had the others heard so much concentrated venom and loathing in one word. 'You come here at a time like this, causing trouble, making accusations you know are not true against our loyal friends. Then when you fail to get your own way you set this creature of yours on Dusty. I think, sir, that you'd better leave the KH and make sure you do not return.'

Lanton's face was suffused with blood, the gash on his cheek showing livid. He rocked back under the impact of the girl's cold fury and contempt. His hands shook and his fat frame quivered with pent up fury. First his plans to get rid of the ranch were all a failure. His attempt to kill the two fighting men and scare off the other riders only partly succeeded. Carron got the rest of the men to leave, but KH still were able to move the herd. Santone's effort had been successful and yet the girls still found the money to meet the note. Lanton guessed Brit knew something about that. Then after his arrival at the KH, Lanton had been humiliated in front of this radiant, beautiful and cultured young woman. His attempts to impress her were gone the same way as the other plans, all because of a small, insignificant young Texas man called Dusty Fog.

'All right,' he snarled back, not able to meet those cold, loathing eyes and feeling about two inches tall before the girl. 'I wanted the KH and was willing to pay a good price for it. I was willing to let your fathers join my Syndicate but they would not have it. Now I'm telling you I mean to have the KH any way I can get it. Either you sell to me or you fight. Make your choice.'

Gloria moved alongside her friend, gripping Rene's arm and feeling the blonde girl was shivering and not from fright. 'All right, Lanton,' she said. 'You've called the play. I'll put it to my ranch crew and we'll tell you our decision. Wait outside.'

Lanton was in control of himself again and mentally kicking himself for having let these people make him lose his temper that way. He knew that there was nothing more he could chance doing now. If he started anything more it would spark off shooting and he would be the first to die. Even though he was unarmed, he knew the Kid was capable of shooting him and saying it was bad marksmanship. Taking out his handkerchief Lanton dabbed the blood from his cheek, looking at it. Then he jerked his head towards the door and led his party outside.

Rene looked at Gloria who turned to face the others. The English girl did not know that there was as much etiquette in starting a western feud as in declaring war between two countries. Gloria knew it and knew she must do this correctly.

'All right, you all heard the man. We can sell to him or stay on. If we stay on we have to fight. The odds are against us and I won't hold it against any of you who want to pull out. I mean to stay and my vote is for war. Brit, this isn't your fight. If you want to pull out——'

'My dear young Miss Knight,' Brit removed his monocle for a better look at her, then screwed it back in again. 'I'm ashamed of you, making such a suggestion before one so young and innocent. Why, damn, I'd rather give up wearing me monocle than desert *you*.'

Gloria's cheeks turned red for she, like the others, noticed the emphasis placed on the last word. To cover her confusion she asked, 'How do you vote then?'

'With you, dear girl. For war.'

'Dusty?' Gloria glanced at the small Texan who was reloading his Colts.

'War!'

'Lon?'

'War,' the word was a Comanche grunt, guttural and hard.

'Mark?'

Mark's eyes went to his cousin's face. 'Need you ask. War.'

'Just?'

'War and I take Brazos' vote. War.' Brazos was in bed still and sleeping off the effects of his wound.

'Rene?'

All eyes went to the beautiful English girl. She stood without a move, her face once more schooled into that composed mask. Her eyes went to each face, knowing her decision would be accepted, even if it was against the majority vote. She did not want to see more violence and bloodshed but in her veins flowed the blood of fighting men, men who were willing to fight and die to protect their own. She looked at the two coffins, in one of which lay her father. He'd fought for this land of his and died for it. She would not allow any man to take it from her.

When she spoke her voice was firm and even.

'War!'

CHAPTER NINE

MARK MEETS FRIENDS

NONE of the others said a word for a moment after Rene spoke. Then Gloria gripped her friend's arm so hard she bruised it. Their eyes met and Rene knew that she'd made the right decision.

'All right, Dusty,' Gloria said. 'You're the foreman, go tell them.'

Dusty turned and walked from the barn, the others watching him go. Brit asked, 'How many men do you think the Syndicate hires?'

'Fair number with the Estradre *vaqueros,*' Gloria answered, her voice bitter. 'I never thought she'd go against me.'

'Well, you figger it this way,' the Kid remarked, looking down at Gloria. 'What would you do if Lanton had your pappy locked in a cellar at the S Star and told you he'd be killed if you didn't join——'

Gloria jumped forward. grabbing the Kid by the arms and shaking him back and forward. 'Is that—— Do you—— How do you—— What——!' she gasped, not able to get a single coherent thought going in her head.

'Easy now, I don't wear a monocle,' the Kid answered and she let loose, blushing furiously. 'I don't know how true it is. Don't even know what it's all about. I don't speak Yaqui sign all that good and we didn't get much time to talk a whole lot. But she told me Lanton's holding her pappy hostage against her good behaviour. I said I'd try and help her first chance I got. That was what I was doing while the rest of you were talking.'

'Yaqui sign. We used to talk it all the time when we were kids. I wondered why old Neety wasn't spouting Spanish at me. Lanton can't speak Spanish and he won't let her.'

'I figgered that out,' the Kid answered modestly. 'One thing though, she allows there's a man with Don Jose all the time, got orders to kill him if there's any attempt at rescuing him.'

Dusty came back from delivering the word to Lanton. 'I don't get it, Miss Estradre looked happier when she left than when she came.'

'Huh, at last we know something the foreman doesn't.' Gloria sniffed. 'Reckon we ought to tell him?'

The two ranchers were buried in the trees beyond the house, the graves having been dug earlier by Mark and Just. The entire crew gathered around the two graves and Brit read the burial service from the Knight family bible. After the graves were filled in Mark drew his right hand gun and fired three shots into the air. Just was holding Rene to him and Brit stood with an arm round Gloria, the other hand gently smoothing her hair.

'We'd best go to the house,' Gloria finally said, drying her tears. 'There's some talking Dusty'll want to do.'

'Sure, he's real good at that,' the Kid agreed.

They all went to the house and Gloria led the way into the sitting-room, waving them into chairs. Brazos came down from the upstairs room where he'd been recuperating. He was informed of the state of affairs and bewailed his luck at missing the sight of Dusty knocking Lanton down and shooting him up.

The Ysabel Kid glanced at the lances and bow over the fireplace and it brought back to him his lodge oath. 'When do I get to take a ride?'

'No you don't,' Gloria snapped, knowing what he meant. 'I'm not having you trailing over the country like a Comanche on a coup taking trip.'

The Ysabel Kid loftily ignored the girl, his eyes on Dusty. There was hope in the Kid's heart, for he knew Dusty would keep him employed as a scout rather than around the house, helping to defend it.

'You haven't many shells for your ride,' Dusty finally reminded him.

'That's right, I haven't,' the Kid sounded exasperated, then looked hopefully at Mark. 'You got any left?'

'The loads in my rifle is about all. I aimed to get some in town but never had the chance.'

'You're near on out, too, Dusty,' the Kid growled.

'I've one box. Old Brazos here uses a Spencer and Brit totes that newfangled centrefire,' Just remarked. 'He's likely got a few rounds but they're no use in the old yellow boy.'

'How about the house, Gloria?' Dusty inquired.

'Pappy and Uncle Mike kept all their bullets locked up in their bedrooms. Me'n Rene'll go see what there is.'

The two girls left the room and Dusty found out how much revolver ammunition the men held amongst them. That was a problem which did not affect either Brazos or the Kid, for they both used cap and ball handguns and poured their powder in straight from the flask. However, the Kid was in need of more powder for his old Dragoon, which used up forty grains at each loading.

Gloria and Rene came back, their faces showing that something was badly wrong. It was Gloria who spoke first. 'Dusty, the box pappy kept the ammunition in has been busted open, it's empty.'

'So is the one in my father's room,' Rene went on. 'You were right, Gloria, we did hear someone while we were preparing the food yesterday.'

'Carron,' the Kid growled. 'I thought his bedroll looked a mite too heavy. Dammit all, Dusty, I should have searched him.'

Dusty did not reply—he was pacing the room. Halting at the table he looked at Gloria. 'Like some paper and a pen, please.'

Gloria fetched them from the office and Dusty sat at the table. He took the pen in his left hand, writing with ease. After a time he looked up. 'Mark, Lon. Can you think of anyone I've missed?'

The other two came and looked at the list, Dusty laid the pen down while the others looked at his neat handwriting. 'Dallas Stoudenmire's down to El Peso,' Mark said at last.

Dusty reached for the pen and this time with his right hand made an addition to the list. Folding the paper he looked up at Mark. 'Take this to town and attend to it. Bring back enough bullets, some lead and powder and any other thing you think we might need.'

'Will it be safe for Mark to go into town alone?' Rene asked.

'Reckon he'll make a good try at it being,' Dusty answered, then gave the girls a significant glance. 'The boys are hungry, you pair of cooks.'

Gloria ignored the hint. She was intrigued as much by the list Dusty had made out as by his ambidextrous prowess. 'What's Mark up to?'

'Why he figgered we'd offended that nice Mr. Lanton and went off to town to apologise to him. Likewise to get better fed than he can get out here.'

Gloria clenched her small fist and waved it under Dusty's nose. 'You listen to me, you shortgrowed, ambidextrous Rio Hondo misfit. You answer up and tell me or I'll hand you your needings. What was on that list?'

'Message to some friends of mine, warning them to stay away from a place where the food's always late,' Dusty answered. 'And don't you go threatening me. I'm not an Earl.'

Both Brit and Gloria looked flustered at this. The young Englishman drawled, 'Dammit Dusty, old chap, you'll be having me think there's something between Gloria and myself.'

'Well, if there isn't now there soon will be,' Dusty replied and ducked as Gloria hurled a bottle of ink at him. It smashed into the door of the cupboard by the fireplace. 'All right, I'll be good. Now, I don't reckon they'll hit at us for a piece. If they do Brit takes the side facing the *bosque* and covers it with his ·44·40. Just takes the back, I'll handle the front and the corrals. Brazos, you being all shot up, take the other side with Gloria to help you.'

'You're forgetting something,' Rene's voice was cool. 'What do I do. Stand in a corner and swoon?'

'And me, although I'd surely admire to go and swoon in a corner with Rene I don't reckon Just would approve,' the Kid went on.

This time it was Rene and Just who looked flustered and confused. Dusty grinned. He'd forgotten the English girl. 'You take charge of all the ammunition. Get all the spare weapons in here with you and the ammunition. Just can show you how to reload them. Then if there is a fight you stand ready to take a gun to anyone who yells for one.'

'And me?' the Ysabel Kid inquired mildly, guessing what was coming.

'Time comes when Mr. Loncey Dalton Ysabel earns his pay,' Dusty replied. 'I want you out there.'

'No, Dusty!' Gloria realised what the words meant. 'It's too dangerous. Lon hasn't enough shells for his rifle.'

'I just want Lon to take a scouting looksee.'

'Won't even take my rifle.'

There was something in the mild way the Kid said this which made Dusty look at his Indian dark friend. The Kid was looking at the display of Comanche war weapons on the wall with a casual, disinterested gaze. Gloria was satisfied. She knew the Kid's reputation as a rifleman and was sure his leaving the rifle behind would keep his mission peaceful. She did not think the Syndicate men could get close enough to the Ysabel Kid to give him the need of a rifle. Without the old yellow boy under his leg the Kid would behave himself, or so she thought.

'All right, come on Rene, let's feed the starving brutes.'

'This month'd be nice,' Dusty answered drily. 'You hands best get started on getting the place ready for a fight.'

The Ysabel Kid and Dusty were left alone in the room. They did not speak for a moment, then Dusty said: 'Be careful, boy.'

'Allus am, aren't I?'

'Nope. Where're you headed?'

'Santone's. If Carron went there he'll have told how we are for shells and they'll be the first to come for us. I just aim to hawgtie them a mite.'

'Best take a rifle then,' Dusty watched the Indian dark face and knew all hell was going to be let loose on the range soon.

'Be dark afore I get there,' the Kid went to the wall and took down the short, immensely powerful bow. It was not strung and he tested the curve, feeling the wood had lost none of its spring and strength. The lack of a string did not worry him, he always carried a length of deer sinew which could be improvised for the purpose of making a bowstring. Then he took the arrows from the quiver. There were five of them, still as bright and true as when first taken and feathered. The points were like needles and the blades almost as sharp as his bowie knife. Slinging the quiver over his shoulder he took the bow down and was about to turn when he looked up at the lance. Deep inside him the Comanche blood stirred. The lance was the weapon of the chosen, the Dog Soldier lodge. His grandfather, Chief Long Walker was a Dog Soldier and in the Kid's veins flowed that same blood. He lifted down the lance. Like the arrows the heavy blade was needle pointed and razor sharp.

'What you fixing in to do?' Dusty inquired.

'I took me a lodge oath to put Santone and Carron under,' the Kid replied. his voice almost mild. 'You wouldn't have a man go back on that, now would you?' He glanced at the door. 'Go make sure Gloria isn't around.'

In the kitchen the two girls were working side by side, preparing a meal for the menfolk. Gloria was looking down at the biscuit mix she was working on when she spoke, 'Rene?'

Deep in thoughts about soft talking, gentle and handsome young men with tragic eyes, Rene looked around. 'Yes, dear?'

'What do you call an Earl's wife.'

Mark Counter rode into Azul Rio town ready for trouble and hoping for it. He headed straight for the hardware store, swinging down from the bloodbay and entering. The owner and his wife were alone inside and both looked brighter at the prospect of a customer. 'Help you, sir?' the man asked, coming forward.

'Why sure. I want six boxes of ·45 Colt bullets. Four Winchester ·44 rimfire, one of the new ·44.40 if you have it. Box of ·52·56 Spencer, some soft lead and a couple of pounds of Du Pont powder.'

The man stared at Mark, his smile dying off as the list got longer.

He glanced at his wife for advice, who nodded, and he went along the shelves collecting the required order. The storekeeper was well aware of what was happening in Azul Rio Basin. Word was going around the town of the deaths of Knight and Hamilton. Also the storekeeper had been in the crowd at Henery's and seen this tall Texas man standing over Speedy Slinger's body. If the Texan rode for KH, Lanton was not going to like his being able to buy ammunition. The Texan was likely not to like not being able to buy it and his dislike was liable to be fast and decisive. Not even the sheriff or the three deputies would be a match for the young man.

Mark could guess what the man was thinking and grinned without much sympathy. The man was in an awkward position as a neutral in the war which was forthcoming. He did not want to cross either side and yet must in the end cross one or both.

The bundle was made up for Mark, who wanted it all in one pile for easier handling. There was quite a large bundle when the man finished and he had to use both hands to heft it. Mark gripped the heavy package in his left hand, paid for his purchases and walked out of the store leaving the man and his wife looking pleased at the sale but also worried in case Lanton heard.

Mark lashed the heavy package to the cantle of his saddle and swung astride without looking down the street. He rode to the telegraph office and left the horse standing at the rail without fastening it. He opened the door and walked in, the old operator glancing up at him, then looking back at the paper he was reading.

Leaning on the counter for a moment Mark looked down at the man. He was a leathery, tanned old timer with hard eyes. Slowly he looked up from under his eye shield, took in every detail of Mark's dress and armament.

'You know Jack Knight, friend?' Mark inquired.

'Might or might not,' the old eyes came up and met Mark's. 'Who is it inquires?'

'Me.'

'Jack Knight hailed from Texas.' It was a statement, not a question. The old-timer knew the range and knew cowhands. He had not been to Henery's after the shooting, but Henery had come across here and told him much.

'So do I. Pappy owns the R over C in the Big Bend country.'

The suspicion died from the old-timer's eyes and he held out his hand. Mark knew he'd called it right. The old-timer was an old friend of the KH and would help them out in their hour of need. He would send these messages for Dusty and keep his mouth shut about them.

Getting up, the old man held out his hand, his face friendly. 'I heard about Jack and Mike. Bad business. How'd it happen?'

'They bushwhacked us, out there on the range. We didn't have a chance to get back at them.'

'Know who did it?'

'Near enough.'

'I'll start getting me mourning clothes out then. Don't reckon you come in here just to make some small talk.'

Mark shook his head, taking out the list and reaching for the pad of telegraph message forms. He wrote on the first form and handed it to the old-timer, who took out his spectacles.

'Dallas Stoudenmire, City Marshal's office, El Peso, Texas——' he read aloud, then stopped, his eyes bulging out. They came out still more when he saw the other forms Mark wrote out. He sent each one off, screwing the form up and tossing it on to the fire as soon as he'd sent off the message.

Mark was aware that this was against the regulations of the telegraph department. He also knew the old man would not pass on what the KH were doing to Lanton. He grinned and winked at Mark. He was supposed to take any message that might interest the Syndicate's boss to the sheriff's office, but did not intend to mention these to anyone.

After paying for the messages Mark stepped out on to the sidewalk and for the first time looked down towards the saloon. Prudence would decree a rapid departure from what might be a dangerous and unfriendly area, but Mark Counter was rarely a prudent young man. There was nothing he would welcome more than a round with the Syndicate men, up to and including the sheriff and his three deputies.

Three horses stood before the saloon hitching rail. Only three. A paint, a black and a claybank. Mark swung up into his saddle, looking again but hardly believing what he was seeing.

'It can't be,' he said, as he started the horse forward. 'It just can't be. But it is.' Riding alongside the three horses he looked down, at the brand on the paint, it was CA. The black carried the Wedge brand. Mark did not bother looking at the claybank. He swung down and fastened his big bloodbay stallion next to the paint. The horse snorted and twisted its head round towards the paint, ears laid back. Then it snorted and settled down again, standing quietly.

Mark stepped on to the porch and looked inside the saloon. There was a mischievous grin on his lips as he watched the three tall young men playing poker dice at the bar. Stepping to the batwings he yelled, 'Draw!'

The one word brought a sudden and instant change to the peaceful scene. The bardog went out of sight behind the bar faster than a prairie dog going into its hole. The other three came round fast, hands dropping hipwards as they fanned out. The slender, pallid young man in the coat went to the right, his ivory handled Colt Civilian Peacemaker coming out ahead of the other two's guns. The tall, handsome blond just turned, his hand dipping and bringing up the matched, staghorn butted Colt Artillery Peacemakers out and lining on the door. The redhead went to the left, his hand making a cavalry twist to lift the walnut gripped Colt Cavalry Peacemakers from where they'd laid, butt forward, in his holsters.

They were around, facing Mark and with guns drawn ready for action in just over a second after his shout.

'Mark,' the handsome boy yelled, his guns making a flashing spin and ending back in his holsters again. 'Yowee, it's Mark. Where's Dusty 'n' Lon?'

Mark crossed the room, hand held out to greet the other three members of Ole Devil's floating outfit. Red Blaze, Dusty's cousin and one-time second-in-command of the Texas Light Cavalry, was almost as tall as Mark. He was wide shouldered, slim of waist and his face was freckled, and handsome in a pugnacious way. His clothes were, like both the others, range style. Around his throat knotted the violently hued bandana Ole Devil gave to him to celebrate his first lone hand chore for the floating outfit.

Doc Leroy was not quite as tall, slender, pallid skinned and looked studious. His name came from the fact that he'd taken some medical training when younger. Now he was known to be able to deliver a baby or set a bone with equal ease and handle anything from taking out a bullet to removing an appendix with the aid of a bowie knife. Doc invariably wore a coat, the right side of which was stitched back to leave clear the butt of his gun.

The last of the trio, Waco, was almost as tall as Mark, wide shouldered, blond and handsome. He looked young, yet his face showed strength, intelligence and self-reliance. His range clothes were clean and neat and around his waist was a Joe Gaylin gunbelt. That told a man who knew the West much about this Texas boy, whose only name was Waco.

Gaylin was an El Peso leatherworker with a reputation which covered the west. He would sell the saddles and boots to any man who could meet his high prices. His gunbelts were something else again. He only made and sold them to men whom he chose as being worthy of the honour. Throughout the west there were probably not more than twenty men who owned such a belt. Dusty and Mark each owned one and those masterpieces of the leatherworker's art gave them that split second of speed so vital. Waco was proud of that Gaylin belt, more proud than of any other thing he owned with the exception of the matched Colts in the holsters. These were a present from the other members of the floating outfit and Waco treasured them.

'Where's Dusty?' he asked again.

Mark grinned. Waco might think of them all as older brothers but it was Dusty who held first claim on the youngster's loyalty. In Waco's eyes Dusty Fog was omnipotent and could do no wrong. Any man who spoke disparagingly of Dusty in Waco's presence was called on to defend himself with fists or guns.

'Out to KH. What are you bunch doing here?'

'Took a herd over to the San Carlos Apache reservation to sell to the Army,' Red explained. 'We figgered you bunch would be done about now and coming back through here, so we pulled in. If you'd rid on we aimed to try and catch up with you. If you hadn't come in we were going to wait for you for a few days.'

'I surely never thought I'd be pleased to see you three hellers.'

'We affects folks that way, don't we, Doc?' Waco

whooped, then leaned across and looked down behind the bar. 'If you all finished playing at gophers, colonel, we'd surely admire to take us another glass of beer.'

The bardog came up, his face sprinkled with sawdust where he'd shoved it down in an attempt to avoid the bullets which should have been flying. Looking at the grinning faces he growled, 'Danged cownurses. Like to scare a man to death with all that fooling.'

'Afore you up and die, lay out four small beers and take something for yourself, friend,' Mark replied. 'We'll have the one, then ride.'

'Sounds like trouble,' Red remarked hopefully.

'Hold hard afore you says a thing, friend. I've got to live here, likewise I was at Henery's this morning,' the bardog interrupted, pouring out the beers and a whisky for himself, then taking the payment Mark offered. 'I mind you and figger what you say to them'd interest Lanton, that being the case I don't aim to hear it. I scare easy and they might want to know what you was saying.'

He winked broadly, raised his glass in a salute, took a sip and went to the other end of the bar to start and polish the glasses with a rag that had seen far better days.

Three faces turned to Mark. Red Blaze was bubbling with eagerness at the prospect of a fight. Waco showed his delight at this opportunity to see some action alongside his hero. Doc Leroy, being slightly older than the other two, was more sober about the business. Mark told quickly what happened to them since their arrival the previous day.

'Sounds like you need us here,' Doc remarked as he finished his drink.

'I'd have surely liked to see Dusty knock that fat hombre down and shoot the gun out of his hand,' Waco went on. 'Can't ole Dusty call his shots?'

Outside the saloon Red glanced at the package behind Mark's cantle and brightened up when told it contained ammunition. 'You got any Spencer hulls there?'

'A box,' Mark replied, warily.

'Good. I've near on run out and——'

'The store's across that way,' Mark finished.

'Why, so it is,' Red eyed the building as if thinking someone built it there to spite him. 'Well what do you know about that?'

'You broke as usual?'

'How'd you guess?' It was a rare thing when Red managed to make his pay last him any length of time.

With a sigh Mark dug some money and passed it to Red. 'Go get another box. The way you throw lead from the rusted up relic you'll need it out there.'

Night was falling as they rode out of town. They exchanged gossip until they reached the rim which overloooked the Azul Rio basin. Then Waco pointed to the north. 'Ain't that a fire there?'

The others looked. In the distance they could see a red glow which grew bigger as they sat their horses and watched.

CHAPTER TEN

THE KID MAKES WAR

THE Ysabel Kid put his left foot against the spur on his right boot and levered at it, working his foot from the leather. He was seated in the barn making preparations for his raid on the Lazy F. Dusty stood by and watched his young friend. It would be dangerous for one lone man but the Syndicate needed to know KH was ready to fight back. The Ysabel Kid was by far the most suited for the task ahead.

'You can still change your mind about the rifle,' he said, taking up the restrung Comanche bow.

'I have. Bow's a fair weapon at close range and makes less noise than a gun. I did some hunting with grandpappy when I went to see him last time.'

Dusty grinned. The Kid liked to visit his grandfather, Chief Long Walker of the Comanches when he got a chance. What he did on those visits the Kid rarely talked about, but Dusty suspected he lived as a member of the tribe.

The Kid took up three of the arrows. He'd fastened a small bundle of tow to the head of each and soaked it in kerosene. He placed the arrows into the quiver and whistled. The big white stallion came towards him. It was not saddled, for leather would creak. In an affair of this kind, the Kid planned, silence was more than golden, it was life itself. Adjusting the Indian style blanket and hackamore the Kid turned to Dusty.

'See if Gloria's anyplace around,' he said. The girl still fondly imagined he was going on a scouting mission.

Dusty looked out through the door but could see no sign of the girl. He turned and told the Kid, who slung the quiver over his left shoulder and the bow over his right. Then taking up the warlance he went to his horse, gripped the mane and vaulted astride with an effortless bound. He lifted the lance in a wild salute and let the horse run from the barn, across the range.

Watching the Kid go Dusty felt uneasy. He knew how well his friend could take care of himself but the lance and bow were poor substitutes for a rifle. True the Kid was still belting his old Dragoon and knife but they were no match for a repeating rifle. However, he knew the Kid meant to go through with whatever plan he'd made and no amount of talk would turn him from his purpose.

Riding at an easy mile-eating lope the Kid looked more Indian than white. His head was bare and his black hair only needed to be taken into braids, and bound back by a headband, for him to pass for a Comanche Dog Soldier. There was a Comanche hardness on his face as he rode with only one purpose, to carry out the lodge oath he'd taken. He sat his big white stallion like a Comanche brave, the heavy warlance in his right hand, butt resting on the toe of his moccasined foot.

It was now that the Ysabel Kid's Indian blood was of most use to him. The Indian instinct for remembering how a new country lay would be of the greatest use to him. Ahead he was making for a strange country and from that view up there on the rim he'd seen enough to give him a fair idea of the lay of the land. The pointed out directions he'd received the previous day helped him in that.

Reaching the banks of the Azul Rio just above where the curve of it formed the north and west lines of the KH the Kid rode slowly along the banks. He found a ford and in the soft earth read a story of a man using it regularly. That would be Carron taking messages to Santone. The Kid hoped he was still at the Lazy F. Crossing the ford he showed caution for he thought Santone might have it guarded. Evidently the rancher thought KH was held down by their lack of ammunition and so it was not worth watching this crossing place.

This was how he wanted things. He did not want to waste any time avoiding guards. Riding the horse through the water he came out on the Lazy F bank and headed across country, following the tracks. Now he was even more Indian than ever. The big white stallion was like a wild creature, the way it moved in silence and was constantly on the alert. The Kid followed the tracks until it was too dark to see them any more. By that time, from a high piece of ground, he'd spotted the lay of the ranch and knew he could find it.

Nearing the ranch he halted his horse against some rocks and through the fast gathering darkness studied the buildings. Lazy F was a bachelor establishment. The house, cowhands quarters and barn were all in one long wooden building. The moon came up while he still watched. Where he was, he faced the barn end of the building and guessed the men bunked in the centre whilst Santone lived at the other end. The barn's hayloft doors were open, a rope still swaying from the pulley. The big, double doors of the barn itself were wide open too. This was as the Kid expected it. The men Santone hired were gunhands, not cowboys, and would not do any more work around the place than they were forced to do.

A small stream ran in a curve around the house, at one side coming fairly close in, at the other being further back, going around the corral. In the corral were horses of the hands. At the very least the Kid knew he could get in and scatter all those horses, temporarily leaving the Lazy F afoot. He hoped to do far more than just that.

There was some coming and going at first around the ranch house and under the moon but the Kid heard the clatter of the cook's triangle and knew the men would be eating soon. He turned and went to where the big white waited for him, quietly grazing. Vaulting afork he lifted the lance from where it leaned by a rock and rode out into the open, the horse treading daintily along until it was halted about a hundred yards from the ranch. The Ysabel Kid slid down, sticking the point of the lance into the soil, then taking the bow from his shoulders and advancing silent as a ghost. He moved in to twenty yards or so of the barn end of the house then halted and froze like a deer sighting a hunter.

All was silent. Not a sign of stirring disturbed the Kid and he took the three special arrows from the quiver, gripping two between his knees. He laid the third on the bowstring and gripped it and the bow in his left hand. Taking out a match with his right he struck it, applying the flame to the kerosene soaked head. Flames licked up greedily over the rag. The Kid drew back the bowstring, aiming at the open hayloft doors. He felt the heat of the flames on his hand, sighted briefly and released. Like a shooting star the arrow curved up, then started to angle down. He watched, hardly breathing as the arrow disappeared into the interior of the hayloft. The second arrow was aimed after the first, but at a slightly different angle. The third, lit and burning, hurled at a lower angle, right through the open barn door to land and bounce into a dirty, hay-littered stall.

For a couple of minutes the Kid stood and watched, waiting to see if the fire arrows were going to work or if he would have to move in on foot and do the lighting himself.

Then he saw a couple of red glows up in the loft as the dry hay caught fire, the flames leaping along faster all the time. Down below he could see another glow as a smaller fire started. He felt the wind on his cheek and could tell it was blowing in towards the barn, helping fan the leaping flames on to the sun dried wood of the building itself.

The Kid felt elated. Unless Santone discovered the fire very soon it would be too late to save either barn or house from complete destruction. The flames were leaping higher now, their crackling sounding even to the Kid's ears. In the corrals the horses caught the scent of the smoke and flames and started to mill nervously, snorting and blowing.

Running back to his horse the Kid vaulted astride and caught up the warlance. The white started forward at a fast run, guided by knee pressure, towards the rear of the corral where the Lazy F remuda were getting more panicky all the time. He was barely there when the door halfway along the building opened and a man came out, making for the corral to see what was disturbing the horses. The Kid flattened along the neck of his big white and waited to see how soon the man would realise the building was on fire.

The man was halfway to the bunkhouse when he heard the crackling and started to turn. As he did so a window smashed in the barn and flames came licking up the wall.

'Fire!' he bawled, turning and running for the barn.

'Fire! All hands and the cook! Roll out!'

Instantly other men started to pour out of the bunkhouse, racing for the barn. The Ysabel Kid's teeth drew back in a savage grimace as he saw one of the men. It was Carron. Just one small matter to be attended to before he left this place.

A slim, dark-dressed man came from the far end of the building, running forward. The Kid recognised this man as the one who threw the dynamite down amongst the KH herd. From the way he gave orders and took command of the situation he would be Santone. Brazos called it right when he blamed the rancher.

The men started to form a bucket chain from the river, using anything which would hold water. They might as well have tried to empty the Rio Grande as stop the raging fire with those few pitiful buckets of water. The barn would definitely be gone and much of the house, for the timber would burn well now and the wind was blowing the flames back along the house.

By this time the horses were wild with terror and racing madly around the confined circle of the corral. The Ysabel Kid watched them and was about to ride to the gate and let them out when he saw a man coming.

Santone had heard the horses and knew they would run themselves to death in their blind panic. He looked around him and saw a man racing by him. 'Carron, go turn the horses loose. We'll get them back tomorrow.'

Like the others Carron was aware of the futility of trying to halt the fire with their few buckets. He wanted to get into the bunkhouse like the other men, and rescue his belongings but a glance at Santone's face warned him. The rancher was angry and liable to start shooting if anyone crossed him. So Carron turned and ran for the corral. He climbed on to the gate and opened it, yelling for the horses. It took time for the wild running animals to find the open gate. When they did they started to stream out and head for safety. Carron watched the horses going by. It would be hell trying to gather them again on foot. The S Star would have to send horses here and help gather the remuda.

The last horse streamed out, Carron dropping down from the gate as the last horse went racing by him. He glanced at the house. The flames were licking back towards the kitchen now and he would have to move fast if he was to save his belongings. He saw something from the corner of his eye and looked around. What he saw stopped him dead in his tracks, bringing him round with his hand dropping towards his gun butt.

Not ten feet away, astride his huge white stallion, sat the Ysabel Kid, lance gripped under his leg, bow raised with the arrow feathers touching his ear, the bow bent so the barbed head was almost touching the wood of the bow itself. Carron's gun came clear of leather but he was too late. The bow string was released and with enough power to sink the shaft flight deep into a bull buffalo the bow hurled its arrow head forward. Carron's eyes bulged out in terror. The arrow point bit through his shirt and the razor edges of it cutting through flesh. through the rib cage and deeper in until the point burst out at the back.

Carron went over backwards, the gun in his hand cracked impotently into the ground. The Kid did not look down. He knew Carron was, if not dead, beyond any aid he could be given out here. Slinging the bow across his shoulders again the Kid took the lance, feeling the rough wood of the shaft in his palm. He turned the white and rode it into the darker area away from the light of the fire.

Santone stood watching the fire, raging at the men who were all busy throwing their thirty-year-gatherings from the bunkhouse. He roared at them to come back to fight the fire but they ignored him. He stood alone at the end of the building, cursing. Then over the sound of the fire and shouting he heard the rapid drumming of hooves.

'Santone!' a voice roared.

Swinging round, Santone faced a terrifying sight. Into the light of the fire tore a huge white stallion looking as savage as a cornered puma, eyes rolling and nostrils flared back. Riding this seventeen-hand apparition was a wild-eyed man in the clothing of a cowhand but with the face of a Comanche Dog Soldier coming to take the white-eye brother's life. In this man's hand, point aiming down at Santone, was the weapon of the dread Dog Soldier lodge, the war lance.

For all his faults Santone was no coward. His hand

dropped fast and the Colt came up, there was only time for one shot, the bullet ripping the black shirt and laying a redhot, bloody, but shallow furrow across the Kid's side. It was doubtful if he even felt the pain as he brought down the lance and drove the point home with a deep-throated Comanche coup-grunt.

Santone dropped his gun, hands clawing weakly and desperately at the haft of the lance. The point went in just below the breast bone, going in to strike and glance from the backbone and emerged at the rear. Santone's feet left the ground. The horse was passing him now and the Kid turned his hand to release the haft. His victim smashed to the ground, the point of the lance sinking into the earth.

At the door of the bunkhouse the other men became aware of this devil rider as he swept towards them. The Kid's old Dragoon was in his hand, his left fanning the hammer back. The gunmen dived in all directions, grabbing at their own guns as the ·44 lead screamed about them. By the time they got their guns out they were too late. The racing white was leaping across the stream as if it wasn't there, its rider laying low along the sleek neck.

Slowly the gunmen came to their feet, all but one of their number. This one was rolling in agony on the floor, his arm all but cut off at the elbow where the soft lead ball struck it.

A big man got to his feet, glancing at the blazing house. Nothing could save it now. He went to where Santone lay on the ground and looked down, the broken teeth in his mouth showing as he made a wry face. 'Who was it?' he asked.

'An Injun looks like,' another man replied, bending over the rancher and trying to raise him.

A buckskin clad old-timer came ambling over from where he'd been bending to take a close look at the tracks made by that racing white stallion. 'Injun,' he grunted in disgust. 'That was no Injun. He was riding a shod hoss. You leave him be. The lance's gone clean through. He's done anyways.'

'What tribe's the lance from?' the big man asked.

'Comanche,' the old-timer replied. 'But that warn't no Injun, Snag. Not pure blood at any rate.'

'He looked like an Injun to me,' Snag Willet growled back.

'Sure and rid like one. Used that lance like a Comanche Dog but he was white, or near enough white.'

At that moment the ammunition left in the bunkhouse part of the building started to explode. The men withdrew fast, heading into the safer area of the open range. One of the men went round to the corral, coming back fast. 'Snag!' he yelled. 'Snag! Carron's dead back there. Got an arrow through him.'

'It was Injuns then,' Willet answered, glaring at the old-timer. 'I said it was, Walpai. It must be a couple of Apaches from off the reservation.'

Walpai grunted. He was a buffalo hunter who was trying his hand at another kind of work as the herds were fast being shot out. He knew Indians better than any man here. 'Apaches don't fight at night. Was I to take money on it I'd say they was Comanches if there was more than one of them.'

'Comanches, you got them on the brain. There ain't any Comanches in New Mexico and you know it.'

'Son, I know Injuns. Apaches, Sioux, Cheyenne, Kiowa. And I know the Comanches too. See that moon up there, Snag. Real pretty, ain't it. You know what they call that moon in Texas. They call it the Comanche moon.'

'Comanches!' Willet spat into the dirt. 'Get the lance out of the boss and we'll bury him and Carron tomorrow.'

Walpai grunted and walked off into the darkness. The other men let him go for they knew his ways. He faded off across the moonlit range to where he'd left his horse and gear cached away. Walpai was superstitious. Twice Comanches had nearly killed him and the wounded man in front of the door had been standing next to him. Three was a bad medicine number for Walpai, the next time might be fatal. He was pulling out before it was too late.

CHAPTER ELEVEN

WACO MAKES A CHARGE

Brit came into the dining-room of the KH and halted by the door. At the table Gloria, Waco, Red and Doc were seated, each with an Indian penny in the right eye in place of a monocle. Brit walked forward to his place, not even showing that he'd noticed them. He reached up, took the monocle out and polished it. Four hands removed the pennies and did the same. Then Brit gripped the cord of his monocle, spun it around and flipped it into his eye.

Four mouths dropped open and four coins fell to the table as the four startled faces turned first to each other, then to Brit. He yawned languidly and surveyed them. 'Let's see you do that,' he said.

The others all howled with laughter. They'd been hoisted by their own petard and were willing to concede him the point. Dusty watched all this with a smile playing on his lips. When the other three members of the floating outfit turned up with Mark on the previous evening—he knew Lanton would soon be starting active hostilities and three more skilled fighting men would be of tremendous use. There'd been an extremely noisy and wild celebration the previous night, the girls agreeing that no disrespect to their dead fathers was meant. It was a strictly sober party but the Texas men did not need whisky to make them enjoy themselves. The three new arrivals were intrigued by Brit's monocle and accent and he was accepted as one of them. This business with the Indian pennies was an attempt to get the better of him. Gloria joined in it for a laugh and to see how Brit could take a joke. The way he'd turned the tables on them did nothing to alter their opinion of him.

Rene and Just came in from the kitchen, carrying a tray

each and putting the food out for the others. Mark and Brazos were the last to make an appearance. The old-timer's arm was still in a sling but Doc Leroy had checked it and was satisfied there was no danger.

'Lon back yet?' Mark asked, looking around the room.

'Sure he is,' Waco answered, indicating an empty chair. 'That's him sat there. Howdy Lon——.'

'Howdy boy, you talking like always.'

The rest of them turned, Dusty throwing back his chair, hands going down towards his guns. The others were staring at the open door and shape in it. Not one of them had heard the Ysabel Kid's return and he'd come to the door silently.

Rene stared at the Kid, looking down at his torn shirt and the bloody graze on his side. 'Lon, you're hurt.'

'Feels that way,' the Kid agreed, knowing the wound was more messy looking than dangerous. He'd hardly noticed it until crossing the Azul Rio and making his long and difficult ride back.

Doc Leroy rose and came forward. He could see there was little need for haste. 'Sit down and I'll have a look at it.'

'Not at the table with the food,' Gloria objected. 'Take him into the office or someplace.'

'Why, thank you most to death, ma'am,' the Kid bowed gracefully and went out with Doc.

The others were all finished eating when Doc and the Kid returned, the latter now wearing a new black shirt. Gloria looked at him as he sat at the table and began to eat. 'See the fire?' she asked.

'Fire?' the Kid was all innocence. 'What fire's that?'

'The fire over at Santone's last night. Brit and I saw it last night as we took a stroll down to the——' Gloria's voice trailed off as she saw the interested looks her cousin and Dusty were giving her. 'I went into the sitting-room and saw the bow, arrows and a lance were gone from the wall.'

'Gone?' there was still innocence in the Kid's voice and expression. 'You mean somebody done snuck in and stole them away?'

'No,' Gloria's voice lifted slightly. 'They got tired of hanging there and got down to go for a walk. What happened?'

Rene provided an interruption. There was a worried look

on her face as she looked down at the empty plates. 'Was it alright?' she inquired.

It was then Gloria realised what was worrying her friend. Rene remembered what her father told her about the adverse comments every cook got. Sipping at the coffee Gloria made a wry face despite the fact that it was strong and well made. 'You sure this is coffee?' she asked. 'I left some dishwashings on the table and this tastes like 'em.'

'Say, Rene,' Waco caught on fast. 'I know us colonials ain't very civilised but there ain't no need to bring ham all the way from England. We've got some here as old and ornery.'

'Eggs aren't cooked enough either,' Dusty went on.

Rene smiled in a superior manner at the others, then turned to Brit. 'Of course one must excuse these colonial cousins of ours. I have some tea in my room, if you'd care for a cup.'

'Of course, dear lady. If Just will give us permission.'

'You go to Santone's, Lon?' Dusty asked and the others were all attention as they waited for the Kid's reply.

'Why sure.'

'See him?'

'Him and Carron both.'

'Carron, huh!' Dusty lounged back in his chair. 'He cashed?'

'Ended that way. You called it right when you said he'd run there.'

'How about Santone?'

'He didn't look any too good. His place got alight somehow. Don't reckon they saved much of it. I took a long way back, hid my tracks some.'

Slowly the full story was dragged from the Kid. Rene watched him in horror almost, wondering how one who looked so young and innocent could be deadly. Passing him in the street as a chance stranger she would have taken him for a pleasant youngster of not more than sixteen. She knew he was far older than sixteen years, that he was savage and dangerous. She also knew his deadliness was an asset to them now. She could feel but little pity for the man who caused her father's death yet she knew Santone died an even more terrible death himself.

'I lost your lance,' the Kid remarked apologetically to Gloria. 'Must have left it lying round someplace.'

'Wouldn't be laying in Santone, would it?' she replied. 'I know what you damned Comanches are when you get a lance in your hands.'

'All right.' Dusty cut across the Ysabel Kid's protests that he was harmless as a newborn babe. 'I reckon Lanton will know about the fire by now and he's likely sent men to help Lazy F. He'll know it was one of us and can make a good guess which one. They're going to hit back at us. Have to or lose face. Brit, you take Cousin Red and Waco and ride the S Star line. Turn back any of them who try and come our way. Just, you, Mark and Lon ride the Lazy F line and do the same.'

'But Lon's wounded,' Rene put it. 'He can't ride with the others.'

'Why surely not,' the Kid agreed with a grin. 'I'll just head up to my bed and——'

'You can stay back here if you want,' Dusty's voice was mild, deceptively mild to one who knew him as well as the Ysabel Kid did. 'I was down to the backhouse and the hole's near to full. You can stay back and dig a nice big, fresh hole if you like.'

The Ysabel Kid came to his feet, making for the door. 'Great climate this. I feel better already. I'll get my hat and boots, then be with you pair.'

'How about us, Dusty?' Gloria asked. 'What do we do while the others are out riding the line?'

'Work on the defences of this place. I'll find you plenty to do, don't you worry about that.'

Brit, Waco and Red rode the banks of the Azul Rio, alert and watchful. The country was scrub and rock covered and would offer them protection if they should find the S Star men. There was only one reasonable ford along this stretch of the river, for the rest it ran deep and fairly fast. Brit brought his horse to a halt near the ford.

'It might be advisable to watch this ford for a time,' he remarked. 'If they're coming, this is where they'll make the crossing.'

The other two agreed with this and led their horses back out of sight. Then they all made their way towards the ford and took cover among the rocks. They were hardly in place when they heard horses approaching and saw a bunch of twenty or so men riding towards the other side of the ford.

'What now, perfessor?' Waco asked.

'Can't have them over here, old chappie. Dusty would never approve. Have to dissuade them. What!'

Red lifted his old Spencer carbine and grinned at Brit. 'You mean shoot at them?'

'Have to warn them first. Wouldn't be sporting to down a sitting bird,' Brit replied, then raised his voice. 'Turn back, you blighters.'

Waco flipped the lever of his Winchester and backed up the shout. 'You do what Brit says. You'll likely offend him if you don't.'

The S Star men brought their horses to a halt, hands grabbing down for their rifles. They did not know how many men were on the other side of the Azul Rio and did not intend making a charge to find out. One of the men brought up his rifle, firing fast. His bullet hit the rock Waco was kneeling behind and the flat bark of Waco's Winchester echoed the shot. The S Star man's hat spun from his head and the others whirled their horses to head for the scrub out of sight.

'Would appear to have gone home,' Brit remarked in a tone which showed annoyance rather than pleasure.

'Nope, they've left their hosses in the trees. They'll be moving in on foot,' Waco answered. 'Look, there's the first of them.'

The S Star men were darting from cover to cover, rifles held ready. One of them flattened down behind a rock and fired at Waco's hiding place.

'Chappies don't appear to like you, Waco,' Brit drawled, his rifle cracking back.

The long range fight was a stalemate on the face of it. From KH's view it was satisfactory apart from the fact that they could not leave the ford. S Star were pinned down on the other side but if the defenders pulled out would be free to cross.

Shoving fresh loads into the breech of his smoking rifle Waco looked across the river. He lined and fired at a man whose shooting was becoming distressingly accurate. The man's shoulder was showing from behind his hiding place and Waco's lead smashed into it.

'How far is it to S Star?'

Brit looked round at Waco. 'Three, four miles.'

'Man'd surely have some sore feet if he walked all that way in high-heeled boots.'

Red glanced at Waco with suspicion. 'What you thinking about, boy?'

'Make 'em walk home. We can't hold them down here for ever and they can waste more shells than we can. I'm going to stampede their horses.'

Brit frowned. 'May I point out their horses are at the other side of the river?'

'Why sure. Good thing I learned to swim.'

'Fool chance your taking, boy,' Red pointed out.

'You got a better idea?'

Red grinned. He knew there would be no point in arguing if Waco's mind was made up. 'All right. Watch yourself, boy, and leave your rifle. I reckon they know how many of us arc here and they'll think things if one rifle stops.'

Waco slid his rifle to Brit and tossed a full box of ·44 rimfire bullets down beside it. Then he slid back from his rock, moving carefully and keeping out of sight of the opposing side. He made his way back to his horse and unfastened the yellow oilskin slicker from his cantle. The yellow fish as it was called by the Texas cowhand, would be of use to him when he swam the river. Moving through the brush towards the river Waco heard the different sounds of three weapons, the deep bellow of Red's old Spencer, the flat crack of his yellow boy and the harder crack of Brit's new model Winchester. The other two were making a very creditable impersonation of three hardy defenders.

At the side of the river he halted and removed the gunbelt to wrap it in his fish. He moved with caution now, looking carefully out over the banks of the river. The S Star were all concentrating their attention on the ford, firing at Brit and Red. Waco listened for a moment, then darted forward and into the water. The river bed fell away sharply here and Waco was swimming almost as soon as he hit the water. Ducking under the surface he swam under water, hindered by the fish wrapped gunbelt. The water ran fast here but Waco was a strong swimmer and found little difficulty in getting across the river.

Waco's head broke water, his every instinct alert. He looked upstream but could see nothing much of the S Star men. The banks here were more open, there was some fifteen feet of grass without cover to be crossed before Waco could get into cover. He came from the water fast and went in trees without attracting the attention of the S Star men. In the trees Waco dropped and lay still, listening. He sat up behind a scrub oak and removed his boots to pour water from them. This was more in the interest of silence than for comfort. Then he unrolled his fish and left it lying under a tree while he strapped on his gunbelt. The fish was waterproofed and kept both gunbelt and Colts dry.

A horse whickered off to the right of him and Waco moved into the trees, avoiding making any sound as he flitted through. He dropped to the ground as he heard the stamping of horses near at hand, crawling forward on his stomach. The S Star horses were bunched in a clearing, fastened to the bushes. A man was standing guard on the horses, his attention to the river and the fight.

The guard was leaning his shoulder against a tree, the stub of a cigarette hanging from the corner of his mouth. He took it from between his lips and stubbed it out, then took out his makings and rolled a fresh smoke. Waco watched the man make his cigarette and stick it into his mouth, then cupping his hands round as he tried to light the smoke.

Waco's right hand Colt came out, the hammer sliding back under his thumb. 'Just hold your hands where they are, friend!'

The man stiffened for a moment, but his control was good and he did not move his hands. He saw the Texan emerge from behind the tree, his clothes dripping water. Wet though he might be, the Texan's gun was lined and showed no sign of wavering. Removing the knife from his pocket Waco flicked the blade open and went crabwise towards the horses, keeping the gunman covered all the time.

The razor sharp knife cut through the reins of the first

horse. Waco moved to the next still keeping the gunman covered. The man stood still, his hands held in front of his face. He was not taking any chance with as efficient acting a young man as this. He stood fast until the last of the horses was cut free.

'Fletch!' a voice yelled and the sound of men approaching came to Waco's ears.

The gunman hurled to one side, his hands dropping towards the butts of his guns. Waco's Colt swung down, following the man as if drawn by a magnet. He released the hammer and saw the man's body jerk under the impact of the heavy bullet. The horses broke at the shot and several men came into the clearing. The young Texan's gun roared out, fanning fast shots across the open at the men. He knew he had to get out of here and fast. The gunmen hit the ground at his first shot but their rifles were lining. A horse raced by Waco, there was neither time nor chance to mount it. His left hand, letting the knife fall, caught the saddlehorn, his left foot hooking into the stirrup.

From behind him he heard shots and the flat slap of bullets as they missed him. One of the shots sent a bullet through the ear of the horse. With a scream of pain the animal hurled right for the trees, going through them as if they were not there. Waco clung on. He'd managed to holster his gun by now and used his right hand to fend off the branches as well as he could. He knew that if he came off the horse he would be under the guns of the S Star men, who were even now racing through the trees and trying to get a clear shot at him.

Then the panic-stricken horse hurled out of the trees and on to the banks of the Azul Rio. Waco was still clinging to the saddle, his shirt ripped and vicious scratches showing where branches had torn at him. He was in worse danger now. The horse saw the river ahead and swung away, heading straight for the ford and the S Star men. They heard the hooves and the shouting, making a shrewd guess what was happening. Men leapt from the safety of the rocks, bringing up their rifles.

Across the river Red and Brit saw Waco's sudden appearance and knew his danger. Their weapons began to crack out, worked as fast as hands could move, pouring lead across at the S Star gunmen. One of the men lining on Waco crumpled and fell, a second hunched forward and went down.

Even with this covering fire Waco was in trouble, the horse was running at full gallop for the ford. He was on the flank away from the river. Kicking free his foot Waco hit the ground, still holding the horn. He came up again in a lithe bound, landing on the saddle. A bullet just missed his head and he saw the shooter knocked staggering by a bullet from Red's old carbine. Then he brought his leg up, over the saddlehorn and kicked his right foot free, leaping from the racing horse. Lighting down on the run Waco dived for the river, bullets tore around him and nothing was ever so pleasant as the water when he felt it close over his head.

Under water he allowed the current to carry him downstream until he was forced to come up for air. The S Star men were watching for him and geysers of water erupted around his head. Hurriedly gulping down fresh air Waco went under again, swimming for the KH shore. He stayed under until he thought his lungs would burst, then came up again, this time getting out of range and striking for the KH bank. A bullet fanned over his head as he dragged himself from the water and to the safety of the scruboaks. There he lay hidden from the S Star men for a time and at last, getting his breath back, he started upstream towards his friends.

Red Blaze looked as Waco dropped alongside him. 'Don't you ever go and pull a fool trick like that again, boy. I wouldn't want to explain to Dusty how you got shot making a raid on S Star and couldn't stop your hoss.'

'Damn fool hoss,' Waco answered, grinning wryly. 'He got a bullet nick and took out like the devil after a yearling.'

From his rock Brit looked Waco over. 'Now I'd have thought you were making a charge at them. You colonial fellers never show any sense. Are you going to tell them, or do I?'

'Hey S Star!' Waco yelled.

'Yeah!'

'I hope you enjoy walking home. Your hosses won't stop running for a week. We're pulling out now. Going to have a ride all the way home. Be there in time for chow.'

An explosive volley of bad language came back across the river. The S Star men were left afoot and faced with a long walk back to their home outfit. A walk which would not be made any easier by the high-heeled boots they were wearing. Any attack on KH was out of the question right now. It would be plain suicide.

'Such language,' Brit called. 'You should be ashamed of yourselves. Come on, chaps. Let's away.'

Lanton paced the room in the S Star that night. His face was pale with rage, the gash on his cheek showing livid and angry. His attempt on the KH was a failure.

'Santone dead!' he bellowed for the tenth time. 'The Lazy F burned to the ground.'

'Didn't do Carron or Holmes any good either,' Painthoss put in with sardonic pleasure. 'They do tell it was an Injun done it.'

'Indian!' Lanton picked the Comanche war lance up from the table. 'It was no Indian. It was that damned, black dressed heller who rides the white stallion. I told Lynch to take a posse from town and bring him in.'

'Townsfolks won't do it, Lanton,' Painthoss looked at Juanita Estradre as she sat reading a book. 'They'll stay neutral in this, more so now they know Cap'n Fog and his pards are siding KH. That gives KH a better than even chance.'

The annoying thing to Lanton was he knew this was true. Lynch was not over-eager at the idea of trying to get a posse of townsmen to help him bring in the Ysabel Kid. He knew that anything less than a small army would have no chance against KH. He also knew the townspeople would not openly take sides either for or against KH. Any attempt to force them into doing such a thing would make S Star more enemies than friends.

'You look like you've bit off more than you can chew.'

'Have I!' Lanton snarled. 'I've told Gogan, Winters and Willet to get word out for more men. Don't you forget I'm running this Syndicate and that the federal law might like to know who you really are.'

Painthoss looked at the fat man. 'One day you're going to push that too far, Lanton. Give this up. Miss Estradre and

I'll let you have the Lazy F and not bother about that agreement that the property of a member of the Syndicate who dies going to the others. You can have both spreads, call off the war with KH and break up the Syndicate.'

'Call off the war?' Lanton's eyes were glaring. 'Never. Did you see the way that girl looked at me. Like I was dirt under her feet. I'll get the KH if it's the last thing I do. I'll take that ranch house, and break them both before I'm done.'

'I've said my piece. You're buying in on more grief than you know,' Painthoss answered and put on his hat.

'Where are you going?'

'Over to my spread. You think over what I've just said.'

Lanton watched the door swing to behind the tall man. He paced the room, seeing again that cold. beautiful face and the loathing in the eyes of the English girl as her tongue lashed at him. He swore even more than ever that he would take the KH, get Rene Hamilton alive and make her bow to his will.

Halting by the table he looked down at Juanita. 'Painthoss does not appear to like our company. At least I'm sure of one of my partners. Aren't I, Juanita dear?'

Juanita followed Lanton's gaze to a strong looking door at the side of the room. She was remembering an Indian dark face with red hazel eyes. A pair of hands moving slowly in the Yaqui sign, promising to try and rescue her father.

Her eyes held hatred of the fat man as she looked up at him. 'Yes, you are. Aren't you?'

CHAPTER TWELVE

RENE FINDS TROUBLE

DUSTY was worried. It was ten days since Lanton's declaration of war on the KH and he knew they could not remain here much longer. There was no reply to any of his messages, not that he expected any. The men who he telegraphed would do what they could for him but it would take time. Ole Devil might be needing his floating outfit at home and Dusty wanted to settle Lanton one way or the other before he left.

The Syndicate men were quiet and had been for a week now. Twice before they'd made attempts at night to raid the KH house but the Ysabel Kid was sleeping days and riding the range by night. One attack he broke up himself with rifle skill and Comanche savagery, the second was handled by the full crew. The S Star gunmen had lost a few men but the KH was untouched by the flying lead.

Gloria knew what was bothering Dusty as she joined him by the corral on the morning of the eleventh day. 'What do you reckon Lanton aims to do, Dusty?'

'Lanton's hiring guns, that's for sure. The Kid's seen some of them coming from town. One of these days he's going to make a hit at us with full strength.'

'You can't stay on indefinitely waiting for it.'

'No, that's what's worrying me. We need every man here at the KH and Uncle Devil wouldn't want us to pull out until this trouble was over and done with. But he may be needing us to home soon——'

'You know we don't aim to leave. I couldn't get those five hellers away from here even if I wanted to. They say they're waiting for the weddings so they can have a good feed.'

'Who's going to get married?' Gloria inquired innocently.

'Well, they do say romance is in the air.'

Before Gloria could frame a suitable reply there was an interruption. Rene and Just came to the corral, the girl wearing a shirtwaist and jeans with a white stetson on her head.

Just caught a gentle dun from the remuda then snaked out his big black. Dusty watched the young cowhand saddling the black and asked, 'You pair riding out?'

'Sure, headed for town. Or on the town trail. We're going up there on the rim to take a look over the basin.'

'Very romantic.' Dusty answered, helping to saddle the dun. He was not any too happy about the girl riding away from the ranch. She could make far too good a hostage if the S Star caught her. However, he knew she and Just wanted to be alone and there was little chance of that at the house.

'We'll be all right, Dusty,' Just remarked. 'There won't be any of the S Star on that side. We'll be back before dark.'

'If you're not we'll be looking for you.'

Just helped Rene mount the dun, then swung into the saddle of his black. They rode off side by side and Gloria asked, 'Ain't love wonderful?'

'They say so. When're you and Brit taking a ride together?'

Rene and Just held their horses to an easy trot until they were well away from the ranch. Then they slowed down and came closer together, yet neither said a word for a time. The girl revelled in the freedom of being astride a good horse again. She loved to ride, although she had not ridden astride for many years. The double-cinched Texas saddle was made in a more comfortable manner than a hunting rig. It was like settling down in a chair and meant for long hours of riding.

'What do you mean to do when the trouble is over here, Just?'

'Been talking some to Brit about it. We figger on going into the cattle business together. I've got about enough money saved to buy a half share in a place.'

Rene felt a momentary panic. She'd grown attracted to this tall, soft-spoken man and knew far more about him now. If he was going into the ranching business he would be leaving this area, for there was no room for any more ranchers in the basin.

'Where will you have your ranch?'

'S Star or Lazy F. Either one will do us if we can get it.'

The girl felt much easier in her mind now. They were the KH's close neighbours. If Just and Brit were only going there they would——

'But the Syndicate owns those two ranches,' she gasped.

'Santone's dead already and I don't think Lanton will be around to stop us. Like the Kid told you there's only one way to handle his kind.'

Rene knew all too well what that was. She could still remember the mad glare in Lanton's eyes and knew he was ruthless, then she remembered the way Dusty Fog could move. That almost unbelievable speed with which he drew and shot his revolvers. After much prodding and pleading on the part of the others Dusty had given her a display of pistol handling which, to her eyes, was nothing short of marvellous. She'd seen trickshot performers who were not as skilled with their special weapons as this soft talking, small and insignificant man from Texas. She also knew that Mark Counter and Waco were almost as fast and good with their guns.

She knew them all very well by now. One minute they were like very mischievous little brothers, the next like big, protecting brothers. In times of danger they were self-reliant, fast-moving, brave and decisive. At other times they acted more like wild, undisciplined boys. Yet through it all one thing remained unchanged, their loyalty to each other and their unswerving devotion to their leader, the Rio Hondo gun-wizard whose name was Dusty Fog.

Once when Dusty was out on the range she'd heard the Kid singing a song, his voice a pleasing tenor. Without thinking what she was doing she began to sing it now:

'He's the fastest gun in Texas and the bravest of them all.
In a street you'd walk right by him for he isn't very tall.
In trouble he's the coolest, fights like a Comanche Dog,
He's from the Rio Hondo and they call him Dusty Fog.'

Riding by the girl Just Smith looked at her and smiled.

He did not mind her singing that song. Dusty Fog was his hero now as he'd been in the days of the Civil War when Just rode with a Georgia Brigade. He was happier now than he'd been for many long years. The Civil War cost his family their fortune and sent Just Smith west with but two skills, horsemanship and the handling of a gun. He'd gone into the trade of cowhand because it offered him freedom and a way of life. Learning his business on a Texas ranch and the great trail drives north had been a hard school. It gave a man many chances to show skill with both horse and gun. It was a way of life which sent many a deep south boy riding the same trail as Jesse Woodson James or Bad Bill Longley. Just was lucky in that he'd never been called on to use his gun apart from in the Concho Sheep war, until this. Now he was fighting to protect someone he loved and who, he hoped, loved him.

It was this feeling of well-being which made Just careless. They were riding on a part of the range where the S Star men would be unlikely to appear and was not as watchful as he should have been. The week of peace lulled him into a sense of false security. He reached for and took Rene's hand in his as they approached a rocky outcrop.

Four men erupted from the rocks, sending their horses leaping forward at Just and the girl. Just saw them too late, his hand going to his gun while his other hand slapped the rump of Rene's horse. Willet was by Just's side, swinging his gun down to smash on to the Texan's hat. Just's last conscious thought was that he'd given Rene a chance to escape, for her horse was leaping forward.

It was there Just reckoned without Rene's breeding and spirit. She did not come from a breed which tamely gave up anything they loved. Taken by surprise by the men's attack she lost control of the horse when it shot forward. Only her superb horsemanship kept her in the saddle until she got the horse under control and looked back. Two of the men were coming after her and she saw Just lying on the ground. She brought her horse in a right turn and headed back for her man, her riding quirt gripped in her hand. One of the men was coming at her, hands reaching out. With grace she avoided his grip and slashed the quirt at him, feeling the hard leather bite into his face.

The man howled, his hands clawing into the air and to his face, the other one spun his horse, but Rene was by him and hurling at Willet. The man who caught the blow from Rene's quirt also swung his horse round, a livid weal along his cheek. He caught up with Rene just as she reached Willet and lashed at him with the quirt. The man swung his fist, smashing it brutally into the back of her head. Rene was knocked from her saddle, the world roaring round as she fell. She felt herself crash to the ground then all went black.

The man dropped from his horse, his face red with anger. He bent over the girl and Willet roared, 'Let her loose, Tom. Get away from her.'

The man looked up at the gun in Willet's hand, lined down on him and snarled, 'She laid a quirt on me. I'll kill——!'

'You'll have to kill me first,' Willet warned. 'This is the gal the boss keeps talking about. We'll take her back with us. Lanton should pay well for her.'

'What about him?' another man asked, pointing to Just Smith.

'Kill him!' The obvious answer came readily from Willet's lips, then he thought again. Even as the man lowered his gun to shoot Willet changed his mind. 'Hold it. We'd best take him along. Likely the boss'll find something to do with him?'

They threw the two unconscious forms across their saddles, then mounting their horses the men headed the range, making for the S Star.

Lanton was standing with his partners on the porch of the S Star house when Snag Willet and the other men came in. The fat man stepped to the edge of the porch, looking at the girl, his eyes narrowing. Moving fast for so fat a man Lanton came off the porch and walked forward to pull the girl's head back and look down.

'What happened, Willet?'

'Caught him and her out on the Azul Rio trail. Thought we'd best bring them both in with us.'

Lanton's face was glowing with hatred and lust as he looked at the girl. 'I wanted to see her. Tell one of the men to get me a buggy ready and take me to town. You'll ride with me. Tell Gogan and Winter I want to see them right away.'

'What's the game, Lanton?' Painthoss came swinging from the porch.

'I'm taking the girl to town. She's going to marry me and we're taking the KH as our home.'

For a moment Painthoss's leathery lack of emotion held, then he snapped: 'Turn her loose or deal me out of the Syndicate.'

'You're forgetting what I know about you?'

'I'm not forgetting. You can do what the hell you like about it. But you let the girl free. I'll be waiting at the Flying P for the law.'

The rancher walked towards his horse and unfastened it. Lanton stood watching, then his hand went under his coat and brought the gun out. Even as he lined the weapon Juanita screamed a warning. With a fast swing Painthoss went up into his saddle and set the spurs to his horse. Lanton's gun swung after the man and cracked. Painthoss felt as if he'd been hit in the shoulder by a red hot iron. He swayed in the saddle but managed to keep on the horse, allowing it to run at full speed out on to the range.

The other men poured from the bunkhouse, yelling and firing after the fast running horse but none of them scored a hit. Willet watched the swaying man. 'Want for me to take the crew after him and finish him off?'

'No need,' Lanton replied, confident in his marksmanship. 'He'll not make it to his spread and I don't want him dead around here.'

In one thing he was right. Painthoss would not get to his spread. He was headed for the Azul Rio and the KH spread beyond it. He did not stop his horse until pain and dizziness made him halt. He stuffed a bandana to his wound, took his rope and lashed himself into the saddle as best he could, then headed on again.

Lanton watched Painthoss's horse carrying into the distance without paying much attention to where it was going. Then he turned and walked back to the porch. His hand swung across Juanita's cheek, knocking her down. 'You lousy greaser bitch!' he snarled and drew back his foot.

Rene groaned, the fat man's foot lowered and he came

forward. Both Rene and Just were recovering. Lanton turned and went into the house, returning with a bottle of laudanum. Removing the cork he forced both Rene and Just to drink enough to keep them out of circulation for some time. A man came up with the buggy ready to travel. Willet and the two tall gunmen with him helped carry both the girl and Just to the buggy and after fastening Just's hands securely dumped him into the back. They laid Rene down by his side and lashed them both into place.

'Gogan, Winter,' Lanton said, turning to the men. 'I want KH taking in the morning. Have you enough men?'

'Got fifty or more,' Gogan answered. 'Say, one of the bunch from the Lazy F was talking about a tunnel that leads to the KH. Carron heard Knight and Hamilton talk about it and tried to find it. He couldn't. If we could find it——!'

'You could get enough men through to take the KH crew. Very interesting. Do you know about this tunnel, Juanita?'

The girl was on her feet again, rubbing her cheek and looking her hatred at him. She did not answer but the look on her face told him all he wanted to know.

'She knows it, boss?' Gogan looked the girl over.

'She does and she'll take you through it.'

'No!' the word was torn from Juanita's throat. 'I won't do it.'

'Yes you will. Gogan, go down into the cellar and work the old greaser over. Don't kill him too quickly.'

Juanita's hand clenched, tears running down her cheeks. She watched the gunman walking towards the cellar where her father was held and gasped, 'All right. I'll take you through.'

'I thought so,' Lanton jeered. 'Keep her here tonight. Tomorrow see she goes through the tunnel first. Then fetch her back here for my wedding celebrations.'

Lanton went to his buggy and climbed aboard. By his side Willet swung into his saddle. They left the ranch and headed for Azul Rio City. Gogan watched them go, then jerked his thumb towards the house. 'Get in there, girl. Don't you try anything. Say, Wint. I was thinking. Those bunch at the KH aren't fools. They'll be expecting an attack at dawn. What I reckon is cut round the back of that bosque in the night and hide out. We'll make the girl take us through on towards noon when they won't be expecting it.'

Lanton brought the buggy into Azul Rio just after dusk. He chose his time with care. There was a new spirit abroad in the town. People were not so willing to accept his domination and they would never agree to his keeping the girl prisoner. He chose the banker's home instead of his more sumptuous dwelling. Ames came to the door at Lanton's knock and looked out, then pulled the door back and allowed Lanton to come in, carrying the girl in his arms. Willet followed with Just Smith hanging over his shoulder.

'Put him in the other room there,' Lanton snapped. 'I'll take the girl into the bedroom upstairs, Ames. Willet, go get the sheriff and the preacher.' Ames led the way upstairs and opened the door into the spare bedroom, waiting until Lanton laid the girl on the bed. She was recovering from the effects of the drug. For a moment her eyes were dazed and dull, then slowly recognition came into them. More than recognition, hatred and loathing.

'Where am I?'

'Safe, my dear. Safe for as long as I make it so. Don't distress yourself. I have a proposal for you. A proposal of marriage.'

'Marriage. To you?' the loathing in her voice made him writhe.

'Yes, consider the advantages of being my wife. Wealth, security, the life of Just Smith.'

'Just!'

'Of course. We have him a prisoner here, securely fastened. Marry me and he goes free.'

She looked at the fat face and shuddered at the expression on it. In the melodramas of the day she'd seen the same sort of situation and thought it laughable. It was not a laughing matter for her now. She knew that to save Just Smith she would make any sacrifice.

'I can't trust you. If I marry you Just will still die.'

'Why should he?' Lanton replied. 'Murder isn't easy to cover up, even out there. I stand to lose far more than I'll gain by killing Smith.'

Rene still did not trust Lanton. There was nothing she could do yet, not if there was to be a chance of escaping and helping Just. 'I'll do it. But if you don't keep your word I'll kill you.'

Lanton smirked at the girl, his satisfaction at having the girl where he wanted her was filling him with delight. 'By the way. One of my men will be with Smith all the time. If you try and escape or raise any alarm the man will shoot Smith through the stomach. Sleep well, my dear. As soon as the preacher arrives we will marry.'

Downstairs Lanton found his plans running into their first snag. The sheriff was there with news.

'Preacher's out of town. Won't be back until dawn, boss,' he said.

'Oh well!' Lanton shrugged. 'One of your men must stay near his house and bring him here as soon as he arrives. The other two stay here, guarding Smith. If the girl tries anything, kill him.'

The sheriff licked his lips, he was looking worried. 'Boss?'

'What is it, Lynch?' Lanton snapped testily.

'Did you go near the livery barn?'

'No, why?'

'It's full of horses. There's some of the best gunhands I've seen in town. They're down at the saloon now.'

Lanton frowned, rubbing his fat jowls. The war with KH had been far from a success although very costly. He might have needed more guns before he heard about the tunnel. Now he did not. They would only be an added expense to be met after the fighting. He could have done with less expenses all along.

'Forget them for now. If our crew can't take the KH we'll take these new men on. Otherwise I don't want them.'

Rene Hamilton was brought down from her room after dawn the following day. Her face was pale but composed as she looked at the preacher, a thin, scared-looking old man. Lanton, Ames, Lynch and Willet were in the room.

'Where is Just?' she asked.

Lanton nodded and Willet held the side door open. Just Smith was fastened in a chair, one of the deputies sitting by him. Rene started forward but Lanton caught her arm and restrained her. The deputy came out of the room at Lanton's sign and shut the door.

'Start the ceremony,' Lanton ordered. 'Are your two men watching outside, Lynch?'

'Sure,' the sheriff agreed. 'I saw to it.'

'Mr. Lanton,' the preacher put in, his face working nervously. 'I will not do this thing.'

'Won't you?' Lynch sneered, catching the old man by the shirt and drawing back his fist.

'Let loose, you brute!' Rene snapped.

Lynch turned to look at Lanton and the fat man nodded. Rene went to the side of the old preacher. 'Do as they say. It will be all right.'

The man looked at her and started to protest but she shook her head gently and went to stand by Lanton. The preacher gulped, then came forward and started to run through the wedding ceremony in a frightened, garbled voice.

Rene stood without hearing what was said, the world roaring around her. She felt Lanton's signet ring slipped on to her finger and the fatal words.

'I now pronounce you man and wife.'

CHAPTER THIRTEEN

THE KID TO THE RESCUE

'AREN'T they back yet?' There was worry in Brazos' voice as he looked out across the range.

'Shucks, you're forgetting when you was young,' Mark replied. 'I bet you never rushed back when you was out with a pretty gal. They'll be back when they're good and ready.'

'I'm worried,' Gloria objected. 'They said they wouldn't be gone for long and it's way past seven now. Dusty, do you think we should send——'

'We got us a caller, not riding too steady either,' the Kid interrupted. 'Looks like that Painthoss gent from the Syndicate.'

The others turned to look. They were down at the corral and had been watching Dusty ride the rough string of the remuda. The Kid's constant vigilance led him to spot the approaching rider. Brazos squinted in the direction the Kid indicated. 'It is Painthoss.'

'Looks like he's been hit!' Dusty barked, then looked across to where Doc Leroy was pitching horseshoes with Waco and Red. 'Doc, we've got work for you to handle.'

Painthoss, hunched up in his saddle, clinging to the horn, brought his horse to a halt and looked with pain-filled eyes down at the men. They and the ranch appeared to be moving, now near, then far away. He felt hands gripping him and unfastening the rope around him. Then he was lifted down, trying to struggle weakly.

Mark lowered the man to the ground and stood back, Doc Leroy bent over, looking down. 'Bullet's still inside. I want him in the house and on a bed. Tote him easy. Mark, Brit, Waco, Red, all of you lift him real easy. He's lost a lot of blood.'

Painthoss opened his eyes, staring wildly around. Then he saw the small Texan called Dusty Fog and knew he'd made it. A feeling of drowsiness welled over him and he almost let himself go. Then he remembered. 'Dusty! They got—— gal—— Smith!'

Dusty's face went hard, his eyes cold and deadly, his hands clenched and he snapped. 'Start catching the hosses, Gloria. We're going to take the S Star apart board by board.'

'Hold hard, boy!' Painthoss's head fell back, his body going limp. Dusty leaned forward, his voice sharp. 'Painthoss. Where is she?'

'No go, Dusty,' Doc interrupted. 'He's unconscious from loss of blood. That bullet'll have to come out and I don't reckon he'll recover consciousness until it has.'

'Get working, then, Doc!' Dusty's voice showed the strain he was under. 'Take him into the house, boys.'

The four men lifted Painthoss carefully and walked crabwise towards the house, carrying the still form between them. Doc headed for the bunkhouse at a run to collect his gear for the task ahead of him. Dusty watched him go, then turned to Gloria. The girl stood rigid, her fists clenched and her face colourless.

'Take the boys, Dusty. Tear Lanton apart, but bring——'

'No, girl! We can't pull out and leave you alone here. Painthoss said they haven't got Rene at the S Star. They're holding her someplace and it could be anywhere. We could ride circles for days and not find her. I'm not taking the boys when they're needed here.'

'To hell with the ranch?' Gloria answered. 'Lanton can have it if he sets Rene and Just free.'

'Which same he won't do. He's holding her and Just for some reason and he wouldn't have sent his men unless he was sure of himself. We've got to wait for Painthoss to tell us where she is. Then we can move.'

'Lanton's sending a tolerable few men here, Dusty.'

The Ysabel Kid watched his friend turn, knowing Dusty was thinking on the same lines and putting the germ of an idea forward.

'Yeah. Happen it'll give you a chance to pry Don Jose Estradre loose. Get to it. Go to the Estradre place first and see the foreman. Tell him all you know. Make him believe you, then bring the Estradre men here to help out.'

The Kid swung towards the corral, taking the rope which hung over the top rail. Dusty raised his voice in a yell which brought Red and Waco on the run. They knew what was wanted and grabbed their ropes to help the Ysabel Kid snake out a relay team of fast horses from the remuda. The Kid left the saddling to the others and ran for the bunk-house, returning with his old yellow boy and a box of Winchester bullets. Dusty was just completing saddling the big white stallion but the Kid took one of the other horses first. He was saving the white for the last, in case speed was needed. Booting the rifle in the white's saddleboot for his friend, Dusty stood back. The rescue of the old rancher was no easy matter. The convincing of a possibly hostile crew as to his peaceful intentions not the least of it. Yet if there was one man who might bring both off Loncey Dalton Ysabel was that man.

With a wild Comanche war scream the Kid sent his four-horse relay racing across the range, riding on a mission of rescue while Dusty set the other men to work. The attack on the KH would find the men ready, willing and eager to meet it. Upstairs Doc Leroy, coat off and sleeves rolled up, worked to save the life and help again to consciousness the only man who could tell them where Lanton was holding Rene Hamilton.

Dawn was just breaking when the Ysabel Kid rode his tired white stallion to the front of the large, stone built old Spanish-style ranch house of the Estradre spread. The ranch crew were gathered outside the house and preparing to start out on their day's work. They were for the most part Mexicans, hard riding young vaqueros, fighting men equalled only by the Texas cowhand. There were a few Americans in the crowd and one of them stood out from the rest, not because he was a tall man, but because, to rangewise eyes, he was the leader.

'Hullo the house,' the Kid called as he rode nearer.

There was little friendliness in the eyes of the men. Their leader, the ranch foreman, grunted. 'You from Lanton. If so go back and tell him we don't want any.'

'I'm not from Lanton,' the Kid replied. 'Got something to

tell you, happen I can set down.'

'Rest your saddle.' The permission to dismount was grudgingly given.

One of the young vaqueros came swaggering forward, hand resting on the hilt of his fighting knife as he looked the Kid over. Glancing at the bowie knife sheathed at the Kid's left side he sniffed. 'Never did I see a *gringo* who could use a knife except to cut his food.'

The Kid turned and looked the young man over in return, then gave a shrug as if the vaquero was of no consequence. In his fluent Spanish he replied, 'You are not old enough to have seen much at all, friend.'

The vaquero's hand brought out his knife fast and drove it towards the black dressed young Texan, meaning at the last instant to swerve it aside in a spectacular near miss. The Mexicans were a nation of knife fighters who knew few peers. The Comanche were also a nation of knife fighters and *they* had no peers at the art of cut and slash. The Mexican struck at a white man but the Ysabel Kid was moving and reacting like a Comanche.

His left arm deflected the vaquero's knife hand upwards; leaving the man's body wide open for a belly wide slash which was the knife fighters *coup-de-grace*. The bowie knife was out and licking forward, eleven and a half inches of razor sharp steel going to sink its two and a half inch width hilt deep into the man's body. Tug Salmon, the ranch foreman, started to jump forward with a yell, but he knew he was too late.

A flicker of amazement and terror crossed the face of the vaquero. He knew he was wide open for a kill. Then something struck him in the stomach, yet it was not the piercing point of that great knife. At the last instant the Kid twisted his hand, the top of the hilt, not the point, jabbing into the man's stomach, bringing a grunt of pain.

The Ysabel Kid moved back, his hands moving, the great knife flying from one to the other in a series of flickering moves as he circled the scared looking young vaquero. Up into the air the knife went, as it fell the Kid's right hand reached for it, missing and letting the hilt slap down into his left. He flipped the knife into the air again, caught it by the blade and thrust it away.

'Reckon that was tolerable for a gringo,' he said casually.

There was a rumble of approval from the watchers and more friendly looks now. The men knew they'd just witnessed a master's display in the noble art of *cuchillo* play. They also knew they were lucky not to be burying young Augustine and respected the Indian-dark young man for his restraint.

'You ain't from the S Star,' Salmon held out his hand. 'Any of that pack'd have killed the boy without thinking twice about it.'

'The name's Loncey Dalton Ysabel. Down in Mexico they call me *él Cabrito*!'

'*El Cabrito?*' Augustine gulped out the words. '*Madre de Dios.* Senor Tug, you are looking at a very foolish man.'

There was once more a rumble of agreement at the words. The Ysabel Kid was well known in Mexico and one of the things which was better known than the rest about him was his skill with a knife.

'Was talking to Miss Estradre a few days back,' the Kid remarked to Salmon. 'I don't reckon any of you know the Yaqui sign?'

'I don't,' Salmon answered. That figured, if the foreman understood Yaqui sign talk Juanita could have got the message to him. 'Any of you know how to make Yaqui sign talk?'

A stocky, leathery vaquero pushed forward. 'I understand it.'

'You new here?' the Kid asked.

'I came from Sonora two days ago,' the man replied.

Slowly the Kid's hand moved, watched by Salmon and the vaquero. This latter's lips moved as he translated the signs into words. At the end Salmon, frowning, asked, 'What's all that about? What did Miss Juanita have to say to you?'

It was the vaquero who replied. 'Don Jose is held prisoner at the S Star, not in Mexico on vacation.'

Salmon looked as if he'd been hit by a club. His mouth fell open and for an instant he was speechless. Then he growled, 'You sure?'

'That's what she told me,' the Kid replied and explained how Lanton would never let the girl speak anything but

English. He told of their meeting at the KH and her use of the Yaqui sign talk to pass the message on to him.

'Saddle up, *pronto, muchascos*!' Salmon bellowed. 'You heard. We're going to pry the boss loose.'

'That's a real smart move,' the Kid sounded mocking and sardonic. 'I told you Miss Juanita talked to me. She said Lanton keeps a man guarding Don Jose all the time. He's got orders to shoot if anybody tried to make a rescue. You go there like you're painted for war and they'll gun the old Don down for sure.'

'All right, you got an idea?'

'Might have. The ranch crew'll all be over the KH, trying to take it. We should be able to get to Don Jose if we works it real nice. What I allow is that we take the crew and leave them well back. Then just you and me ride on in. After that we'll have to play 'em as they fall.'

'That hoss of your'n looks to have been well rid. Take your pick of the remuda.'

The Kid nodded gratefully and went with the ranch crew to the corral and looked over the remuda. He picked a fast-looking leggy roan with a mean glint in its eyes. The rope made a fast hooleyann throw and brought the horse out. Eager hands saddled it for the Kid and he went up astride with a bound. The horse was a fighter, one which would give its last ounce of endurance to any one man who could master it. The men watched as the Ysabel Kid, riding like a demon, fought the horse out. They admired the iron guts of a man who could ride all night and still choose a bad horse because it would give him the speed and endurance he needed.

The Estradre crew collected their own horses in record time and lit out across the range. The big white stallion stood snorting and watching them go, then like a faithful dog set out at an easier pace following its fast riding master.

Lanton's cook sat in the sacred precincts of the ranch dining-room, feet on the polished table top. Between his lips was a big, costly cigar and by his side a bottle of finest bonded whisky. He was at peace with the world, for while the crew and his boss were away he was making the most of it. The men, less two guarding the old prisoner in the cellar, had pulled out on the raid and he'd been left to make a search of the house. The cigars and whisky came from Lanton's private office and the fat cook was making the most of his leisure. He glanced at the door at the room side. If one of the guards came up through it, he would have to hide the plunder and make out he was cleaning the dining-room.

The morning sun came through the window behind the cook, filling him with a gentle glow of well-being. It was pleasant just sitting here and his head nodded forward towards his chest. Then suddenly somebody shook him. He opened his eyes, ready to splutter out excuses. His eyes met two of the coldest, cruellest eyes he'd ever seen, red hazel eyes that seemed to bite down into him, no mercy in them. The face above him was not belonging to any man of the S Star crew. It was a dark, innocent-looking face, but those eyes were far from innocent.

'Rest easy, friend,' the voice was soft, cold and mocking.

The cook sat up, looking wildly around him, first at the black dressed, dark-faced boy, then at Tug Salmon. The latter was smiling, although the smile did not reach his eyes.

'Howdy coosie!' Salmon greeted. 'Where's the crew at?'

'Out on the range, working,' the cook replied, shooting a nervous glance at the cellar door. 'What you doing up this ways, Tug?'

'Come over to see Miss Juanita, her not having been to the spread for a few days. We lost some stock to rustlers and want to know if she wants us to take out after them.'

'She went to town with the boss.' Once more the cook looked at the cellar door. 'She won't be back today so you best take out after them without her knowing.'

'Yeah!' Salmon looked around the room with casual interest. 'You boys at S Star sure have it good if this's the cookshack. You don't have it like this over to home.'

'We don't either. I was just cleaning up in here when I got a touch of the grippe and sat down to ease myself,' the cook answered, looking again at the Ysabel Kid. 'Don't recollect seeing you at Estradre's before, friend.'

'Just took on. The name's Comanche Blood.'

The Kid knew he'd made a bad mistake the moment he said his favourite alias. Every man of Syndicate knew which tribe was blamed for the death of Santone and Carron. The Kid cursed himself for leaving the arrow lance, although there was no way he could have recovered either during the few wild minutes at the Lazy F. He saw the cook's eyes again flicker towards the door. For a moment the man appeared to be on the verge of shouting out but thought better of it.

Walking to the window the Ysabel Kid looked out at the corral. 'You either hold a real big remuda or the hands aren't using their strings,' he marked, for there were many horses moving around.

'Sure,' the cook felt nervous. He knew the Kid knew a working cowhand would take his string along. 'The boys aren't far out, just over to the lower forty. They come back when they want a change.'

Once more the Kid moved, prowling around the room, looking things over until he halted by the door. He could hear the cook's breathing grow louder but did not turn around. 'Real strong looking door to be inside a house, Tug,' he marked. 'I'll bet it's real, genuine oak.'

With these words the Kid lifted his hand, banging on the door twice, hard. Then he flattened himself against the side of the wall, eyes on the handle of the door, knowing it would open away from him.

The cook came to his feet, his mouth opening to yell a warning. Then he felt something touch his temple and turned his head. The muzzle of Tug Salmon's long barrelled Colt poked the cook in the eye.

'Sit fast, coosie. We know who's down there and we're going to get him out.'

In the cellar two men sat at a table playing cards by the light of a lantern. Seated on a bed at the side of the small room a tall, slender, grey haired man, wearing the clothes of a Mexican hidalgo, sat reading a book by the light which came through the small window at ground level.

The cellar had been blown into the solid rock under the ranch. It was a small room, although fairly comfortable. Lit only by the lamp on the table and the small window and poorly ventilated, it was still habitable and Don Jose Estradre was not showing any signs of ill-treatment or ill-health through his imprisonment.

When the two knocks sounded the gunmen looked at each other, coming to their feet. One glanced at Estradre but the old man still sat reading his book and ignoring them.

'It must be that damned fool cook,' the taller of the men growled.

'Yeah. You watch the old man while I go and take a looksee.'

The only way out of the cellar was up a flight of steps cut into the rock, leading to a platform and the door which opened in from the dining-room. The gunman went up the steps, hand on gun, even though he was sure it would only be the cook knocking. Gripping the door handle he pulled and the door swung towards him. Not seeing the cook he lifted his gun out and very cautiously started to look out of the opening.

The Ysabel Kid watched the door opening, hardly breathing, tense and ready to move as a hungry cougar lying on a limb above a whitetail decr. The man's head came into view like a turtle taking a look out at the world. Lunging forward the Kid's hands gripped the gunman by his hair and heaved. It was no time for fancy fighting. The man howled as he felt the pain. It was as if some Indian was trying to pluck his scalp out without making the knifecut first. With a startled yell he shot from the door and across the room like a cork out of a bottle.

The Kid did not wait. He saw the cook knock up Salmon's gunhand, then grapple with the ranch foreman. Then the Kid was through the door and on the small platform above the cellar.

At the bottom of the steps the second gunman whirled from where he stood looking up. His gun came out and started to swing into line on the old Mexican. The Ysabel Kid saw all this and acted with Indian wild speed. From his lips came a Comanche war-scream which would have scared a tobacco store wooden Indian into dropping his cigars. His razor-edged bowie knife was in his hand as he hurled himself out into space and down at the man. The gunman panicked for a vital instant. The yell shook him and paralysed him for that split second the Kid needed. The gunman hesitated as to his action, whether to down the old

Mexican first or deal with the new and more deadly menace. His instincts told him he must kill this knife-toting stranger first, then he could drop the old man.

But by the time the decision was made it was already too late. The gunman's gun was harmlessly pointing away from both the Kid and Estradre when the black dressed boy crashed full on to his body. They went down, the gunman's gun sent a bullet into the wall. Then he felt something strike his side. For an instant agony filled him, then a dull numbness. His hand relaxed and the gun fell to the floor.

The Ysabel Kid rolled from the man, coming to his feet fast, the length of his bowie's blade dripping blood. He heard a sound and looked up to where the second gunman stood, lining his Colt down. Lunging forward the Kid knocked Estradre aside, pushing the old man into a corner. In a continuation of the same move, the Ysabel Kid dived the other way, right hand dropping the knife and twisting back around the butt of his gun. The bullet hit the bed between the two men even as they separated. The Kid twisted in the air and landing started to fan his old Colt's hammer as fast as he could, throwing lead up in the general direction of the platform. He shot, not for effect but to throw the other man off his aim. Flame and smoke belched from the yawning ·44 bore of the old Dragoon. The gunman took an involuntary step back as the soft lead balls howled up, his eyes trying to pierce the smoke which lay like a fog below and hid the two men from his view.

That was what the Ysabel Kid hoped would happen, he knew that while fanning could be deadly done by an expert at close range, he was not expert enough to get a hit at that distance. His intention was both to prevent the gunman from getting a clear shot, and try to hide under the swinging powder smoke. Five shots he fanned off, the explosions booming loud in the room, their concussion putting out the lamp. Then he held his fire, for he had only one more bullet left in the old gun and his powder flask was in Nigger's saddlebag. It was one of the rare occasions when the Kid would have preferred to be holding a cartridge loading gun instead of his old four-pounder thumbuster.

The gunman looked down, knew the game was up and turned to run. He came through the door, swinging his gun towards the two struggling men. Tug Salmon saw the man emerge and with a surge of his muscles threw the cook backwards, right into the bullet the gunman threw at him. Salmon went to the floor in a dive, landing and firing two fast shots. The first made a hole in the wall an inch from the gunman, the second from the swinging barrel stiffened the hired gun up, a hole appearing in the centre of his shirt. He staggered back to the wall and a third bullet brought him sliding down to sit in a lifeless huddle.

Hurdling the groaning cook Salmon ran to the door of the cellar, the whirling smoke was eddying up and he yelled. 'You all right, boss?'

Two coughing shapes came up through the smoke, Estradre leaning on the Ysabel Kid's arm and trying to wipe powder-induced tears from his eyes. The Kid lowered the hammer of his old gun and grinned at Salmon. 'Lucky you yelled, I was all set to shoot.'

Salmon leapt forward to help his boss up the steps and the Kid returned into the smoke to fetch his knife. He came up again and wiped the blade on the shoulder of the dead man with Comanche indifference. Then he looked to where Salmon was helping Estradre into a chair and pouring out a drink from Lanton's best bottle.

'You all right, boss?' Salmon asked. 'When I heard that damned yell I thought they'd got you for sure.'

'I was close, Tug. Very close. This young man arrived only just in time.'

'They treat you all right?' Salmon glared at the cook, debating what action to take if his boss gave a negative answer.

'Well enough. I lack for exercise, that is all. Where is Juanita now?'

The Ysabel Kid went forward, rolling the cook from hands and knees on to his back and looking down. 'Where is she, *hombre*?'

The cook looked up again. Those eyes were even more savage now and he could not think how he ever felt that was an innocent face. 'To KH!' he screamed. 'Get me a doctor.'

'To KH?' the Kid growled. 'Why'd they take her with them?'

'She knows a tunnel that'll take them into the house.'

The Kid slammed the man's head back to the floor and got up. A tunnel leading to the KH house. What a fool he'd been. Nearly every old Spanish style house had such a thing, a precaution against attack. His knife came out and it took all his willpower to prevent the blade sinking into the cook. He shoved the knife away and turned to Estradre.

'I ride to KH. Do I ride alone?'

CHAPTER FOURTEEN

THE FIGHT FOR KH

THE lights were still burning at the KH even though the hour was long past midnight. Outside Waco and Red were patrolling, alert and watchful. In the house the others waited for Doc Leroy to give the word that Painthoss could speak and tell them what they needed to know. Gloria, face lined with anxiety, kept the coffee pot boiling for the men. Brazos was with her, his old face lined and looking even older. In the days since her arrival Rene had become as dear to the old-timer as Gloria was.

Waco came in from his patrol and took the steaming cup of black coffee the girl offered. He looked down at her and grinned. 'Now don't you go to worrying. It'll be all right.'

'It's easy for you to talk!' Gloria snapped, then by a conscious effort got hold of herself again. She knew Waco was only trying to cheer her up. 'I'm sorry, Waco. It's——'

'What about? Sure it's easy for me to talk. I learned real young and learned real good.'

Dusty and Mark entered the kitchen and looked at the clock on the wall. The fingers were pointing to half-past three. Mark came to the girl and dropped a hand on her shoulder. 'Nothing yet, redtop. Dusty, I still allow we should head for town.'

'He'll likely be there,' Dusty agreed. 'But this is one time we daren't take chances. It isn't just a straight swap Lanton's after or we'd have heard from him before now. I'd take a chance and send the boys to make a search of every place they might be holding her but there isn't the time and we need them all here. It's no use you and me riding off half cocked to the town then Painthoss recovering and telling Doc they're holding her some other place.'

'You take all the boys if you want,' Gloria gasped. 'I don't care what happens to the ranch if we get Rene back safe.'

'It's not that easy, Gloria,' Dusty answered. 'Lanton's got her and he's got more in mind than a straight swap, her for the KH. If that was his idea we'd have heard from him by now. He'd want us to know and make a deal before we could think out a move against him. Besides, Painthoss isn't any kind of saint. He'd have stood for a straight swap, but not for——'

Dusty rose and paced the room, his mind working furiously. He was trying to put himself into Lanton's place, to think as the fat man would be thinking. He came to a halt, the others saw the change in him, his hands dropping towards the guns at his side, cold murder in his eyes.

'What is it, Dusty?' Gloria was suddenly afraid.

'Mark, go see Doc. If Painthoss can't talk we're going to town without waiting any longer.'

'Why?' Mark asked. He was scared, too, for he'd never seen Dusty so dangerous.

'Lanton aims to marry Rene.'

'Why should he?' Gloria gasped. 'She'd never do it.'

'She'll do it, gal. What'd you do happen you were in the same predicament and Lanton told you it was marry him, or Brit's life?'

For once the girl did not howl out at the reference to herself and Brit. She knew there was only one thing she would do. 'You're right. I'd do it and so would she.'

'Why'd he want to make her marry him?' Mark asked.

'Remember in the barn. She made him look two inches tall when she called him down. This's the way of getting his own back on her.'

Doc came in. 'Dusty, he's awake, but he's dead weak. Should be sleeping but he won't until he's seen you.'

Dusty went upstairs fast, followed by Mark and the girl. They entered what had been Knight's bedroom. Painthoss lay in the bed, his face colourless but his eyes were bright. 'They took the gal to town, Cap'n Fog,' he said. 'He's going to make her marry him. I've been bad in my time but I wouldn't stand for that. I was coming here to warn you. Forgot Lanton's lil stingy gun. Young Juanita yelled a warning. He winged me but I still came here to warn you.

That gal's sure got Lanton fooled, I saw her wigwagging to the Kid but I don't know the signtalk she was using.'

'You get to sleep, *amigo*,' Dusty ordered, 'and ole Doc'll do all he can for you.'

'Lanton's men'll be here in the morning. Happen you send word, I've got eight men who'd be more'n pleased to take sides with you against Lanton and his guns.'

'No time to fetch them and I haven't a man to spare,' Dusty replied, he held out his hand. 'Thanks for the offer.'

'You know me?' Painthoss asked as Dusty turned to go.

'Knew a man like you once. He's dead now. Fact being my pappy'll be sending out word that Cullen Baker's dead and the law might as well rip up their dodgers on him. Lanton'd hold a thing like that over a man's head if he knew about it.'

Painthoss's face showed his gratitude. A law man of the reputation of Dusty's father, Hondo Fog, had influence. If he said the old-time Texas outlaw, Cullen Baker, was dead, others would believe it. Painthoss could look ahead to a life of peace.

'Where're you going, Dusty?' he asked.

'To town, Mark and me.'

'Give 'em hell, boy.'

Dusty Fog and Mark Counter went downstairs again and into the kitchen. They took out their guns and checked them over, examining the loads. Gloria watched them, her hands clenching and unclenching again. Brit came and stood by her, taking her hand in his and squeezing it gently.

'Take Waco and some of the others,' she said.

'Nope, you'll want them all here,' Dusty answered. Red was here now and the men of the KH looked to Dusty for orders. He told them what he knew and the angry, almost animal growls of the young men came to his ears. 'The rest of you'll stay here, Brit, I'm leaving you in command.'

There was no time for the others to say anything for Dusty was already walking to the door. Brit opened his mouth to object, then closed it once more. He was an Army man who knew the value of obedience to orders. He followed Dusty and Mark out to the corral where they saddled their horses. 'Any orders, Captain?'

'Sure, turn the remuda loose, scatter them. Waco's paint'll come back to him when he whistles. Anyways we'll be back in time to help you bring the horses back in. Then get the house ready. They'll likely attack at dawn, don't rely on it. If they aren't here at dawn, don't count on their not coming at all.'

Mark and Dusty swung into their saddles. Mark leaned down and gripped Brit's hand. 'Take care of ole redtop, Brit. Tell her we'll fetch Rene back here unmarried.'

'Or a widow,' finished Dusty Fog, then horses were running for town.

Brit returned to the kitchen and looked at the circle of anxious faces. 'First,' he said, 'I'd like to say I don't approve of being placed in command and feel it would be more in the democratic principles of you colonials to put it to vote who leads us.'

Waco grinned back at the tanned young Englishman. 'Ole Dusty, he done held him an election, took a vote and he voted it unanimous that you takes over us colonials.'

'And ole Dusty's like to get real mean if he don't get his way. I reckon his mammy spoiled him when he was young,' Red went on.

The men were solidly behind Dusty's decision to place Brit in charge of the ranch. Waco and Red were fighting men from soda to hock but they knew they were reckless and needed a steadier hand to guide them. Doc was slightly older but he would be too busy handling any wounded to take control of the others. Brazos never thought of himself as a leader, and he was more than willing to let Brit give the orders.

'All right, chaps, get to it. I want the remuda scattering. Then we need some rest. We'll have one man in Painthoss's room to keep watch and also to keep an eye on Doc's patient. There are two windows in the room which cover the front of the house and the corrals, the other the *bosque*.'

'Two of us watching might be better. The windows in my room at the back of the house covers the other two sides,' Gloria remarked.

'Not having entrance to your boudoir, Gloria, I wouldn't know about it.' Brit ignored the sniggers of the other men.

'Waco, get the remuda out and away. Doc, you and I will take the first watch. You take the front and I'll take the rear. The rest of you get some sleep.'

The group broke up, heading for the different duties or to try and snatch some rest. Brit waited for Waco to return from scattering the remuda then they made a round of the house to make sure all was secure.

The sun was high in the heavens when Gloria woke, laying fully dressed on the bed in Hamilton's room. She had hardly slept until the first light of morning. Sitting up it took her a moment to remember where she was and what was happening. She went to the door and made her way downstairs to the kitchen. All the men except for Red were seated at the table, eating a meal. Brit rose as she entered and pulled out a chair for her.

'Take a pew, dear girl. Brazos is cook today. We've elected him as he's been riding in the wagon for days now. Do the old blighter good to have some work.'

'Didn't they come?' she asked, looking around.

'Sure,' Waco jeered. 'They's come, we shot them all, they shot us all. Then they lit out and we let you sleep through it all.'

'You can tell she's kin to ole Mark,' Doc remarked. 'All that clan can sleep.'

Gloria made a rude noise through her lips, then sat at the table next to Brit and ate her breakfast. Pushing back her plate she looked at him. 'What's worrying you?'

'S Star. Their tactics should have been a dawn attack. They didn't come. I can't understand it. Painthoss was sure they'd be here.'

'It could be a trap.'

'Why sure,' Waco scoffed. 'Ole Painthoss, he says to Lanton. "Let's us lay a trap for KH. Just you sorta shoot me in the shoulder and I'll head across the KH bleeding like a throatcut shoat——"'

'Thereby raising all kinds of fear and false apprehension amongst them,' Brit interrupted Waco, watching the anger rising the colour in Gloria's face. 'It could have happened, although I gravely doubt it.'

'So do I,' Gloria answered, holding her voice to a fair imitation of his accent. 'Actually, old chappie.'

Time dragged by without any sign of the S Star men. Brit kept his men on the alert all the time. However, he did not mean to relax, for he remembered what Dusty told him.

Just before noon Gloria took a coffee pot and went the rounds of the men. Waco was in the bunkhouse room, covering the forge and backhouse. Brit and Doc in the sitting-room, by the windows. Brazos in the kitchen and covering the other side. She went upstairs and entered the room where Painthoss lay in his bed, eyeing Red Blaze who was moving between the two windows. The rancher tried to sit up, fuming at his inability to get up and help the KH fight off the attack when it came.

'Look,' his voice held some of its old paw and bellow. 'I fit Injuns and Yankees, I've been wounded wuss than this itty bitty scratch. Gimme a rifle, Miss Knight and I'll get up——'

'And fall right down again,' Gloria answered. 'Doc says you stop in bed and stop you will.'

Painthoss knew he was more of a liability than an asset to the defenders of the house if he was on his feet. He did not mean to give up his attempt to help without a struggle. Then he saw Red Blaze standing behind the girl, holding an old Spencer carbine which he waggled derisively at the rancher and made gestures as if he was shooting from the window.

'Then get that red topped heller out of here!' Painthoss howled like a trap-caught wolf. 'He keeps riling me. Just look at him.'

Gloria swung around but Red was making a very creditable picture of a keen and alert sentry. She turned back to the bed; and swung back fast to catch Red once more making more signs. She grabbed up a boot and hurled it with a good aim right at Red's head. He ducked and grinned. 'All right, I'll be good.'

Gloria left the room and went to the sitting-room downstairs. She found Brit at the table loading a spare rifle. For once his monocle was not in his eye. It lay on the table and she saw the chance to do what she'd wanted to ever since she met him. Going forward she picked up the monocle and looked through it. 'You old faker. It's plain glass.'

'Of course,' Brit did not appear to be distressed, 'a chappie has to have a monocle, don't you know.'

From upstairs they heard the bellow of Red's Spencer, at the same moment the windows of their room burst and bullets smashed into walls. Brit caught the girl's arm and thrust her to the floor. He caught up his rifle and dived across the room to where Doc was already in place and looking out.

'They're in the *bosque*,' Doc remarked. 'Fair slew of them from all I can see.'

Brit flattened himself against the wall, looking out. Lead still came slashing at the house from the trees. 'Strange, I can't see what they hope to gain by this. They can't get at us across that open land. Two hundred or more yards without cover and faced with men who can handle rifles.'

'Likely we'll soon find out,' Doc answered.

Juanita Estradre stood beside the leaders of the Star hired guns. Gogan looked down at her and gave her a shove towards the opening of the tunnel his men had just uncovered. 'Get going. You start the boys shooting at KH, Winter. We'll likely be making some noise in that tunnel and it'll help cover us.'

Winter walked away to give his orders. Even as Juanita walked towards the dark opening she heard the crack of rifles and knew the KH were fighting with no knowledge of their danger. 'It is many years since I last used the tunnel,' she said. 'It may be blocked.'

'You'd better start in to praying it ain't.'

Pushing the girl forward Gogan took a ten gauge shotgun from one of the men standing by. At the mouth of the tunnel were six more men, each with a double barrelled gun in addition to his armament. The KH crew were not to be taken prisoners, they were to be killed on the spot. A ten gauge at close quarters was the best weapon for such a task.

'Time we got moving,' Gogan told his men. 'Get in there, gal.'

Juanita led the way into the old tunnel. The walls were crumbling and the timbers rotten with age. At her back the seven men moved cautiously, watching they did not crash into those rotted timbers. Juanita was tempted to throw herself at the wall in a desperate attempt to bring them crashing down on the attackers behind her. Common sense warned her of the folly of such an action. She might not be able to fetch the tunnel down and the men could find their own way from here to KH. Her only chance was to lead the way and warn her friend, even if she died after doing it.

Gogan lit a lantern and in the faint glow she could see better where she was going. The walls were even worse further in and they stopped once as dirt trickled down from a beam. A gunman gulped and whispered, 'This's too damned dangerous.'

Moving on again the girl saw and felt the tunnel after going downwards, starting to rise again. In the light of the lantern she saw a square of wood and the end of the tunnel ahead. The wooden square was the trapdoor which led into a cupboard of the KH sitting-room. It had never been fastened in the old days and Jack Knight always kept the hinges well greased. She did not know if the same still held good.

'There it is,' a man hissed.

'Sure. Ladies first!' Gogan waved Juanita on, he'd been given certain orders about her. She was not to get away alive.

Juanita reached up and pushed on the wood. It gave and she knew the trapdoor was not fastened. Slowly she forced it up, feeling a pair of boots or something sliding down. Now, faintly, she could hear the crack of rifles and knew at least one of the defenders was in the sitting-room. Behind her Gogan eared back the hammers of his shotgun ready. He could hear the shooting and knew Winter was doing his share by distracting the KH from any slight noise the attacking force might make.

Gripping the edge of the trapdoor Juanita pulled herself up, swinging around to sit on the edge, then get to her feet. Gogan's face lifted up over the edge. It was the time Juanita had waited for.

'Pig!' she hissed and kicked the man full in the face.

Even as Gogan gave a startled yell and fell backwards the girl turned, she flung herself back at the cupboard door. The door opened and Juanita went into the room fast. She saw two men and Gloria by the side of the window, they turned with startled expressions, staring at the dirty vision.

'*Pronto Rojo!*' Juanita screamed, falling to her knees.

Behind Juanita Gogan's face appeared above the edge of the trapdoor. He was mouthing curses as he tried to bring the shotgun up to kill the girl who'd betrayed him. Doc Leroy took a hand. Like the others he'd been taken by surprise by the sudden appearance but he reacted faster. There was not time to bring round his rifle so he dropped it, throwing himself forward. The boneless looking right had made a flicker, the shiny ivory butted Colt in it and roaring even as he landed.

Gogan's head rocked back, falling out of sight. His cocked shotgun exploded as he landed, the charge tearing into the man behind him. This man's own weapon roared and then with a low rumble the roof and walls of the tunnel collapsed.

Doc Leroy was hurling himself forward, his Colt ready to fire on the next man from the trapdoor. He heard the rumbling and saw a cloud of dust roll up from the hole. Moving nearer he looked down, Gogan lay half buried under the earth but there was no tunnel any more, the concussion of the explosion having brought it down.

Shutting the trapdoor down Doc turned to look at the two scared faced girls. It was Gloria who asked, 'What happened?'

'The shotguns brought the roof down,' Doc answered. 'Damn it to hell, why didn't I think of the old tunnel?'

'Yeah,' Gloria's voice was flinty. 'I should have thought of it, too. How'd they hear about it?'

'Carron heard your father talk of it,' Juanita's answer was stiff.

'That figgers, although anyone who knows these old Spanish places would know about a tunnel. There's one at your place. And don't you worry about Don Jose, Neety. The Kid's gone to rescue him, after Painthoss came to warn us.'

The shooting from the woods was stopped as the men went to see what caused that rumbling from the tunnel. Juanita and Gloria stood facing each other and would have been in some considerable danger if the men were still shooting through the KH windows.

'Painthoss?' Juanita gasped. 'But Lanton shot him.'

'He made it here.' Doc remarked. 'Likely live, he's a hard old cuss.'

'He was not a willing member of the Syndicate. Lanton held something over his head. Something to do with his past,' Juanita told her friend. 'I forgot Lanton took your friend to town and——'

'We know that too. Dusty and Mark went after her. They'll bring her back safe enough.'

The two girls hugged each other, their faces radiant and happy now. Brit watched them for a moment, then glanced from the window and remarked: 'I hate to break up your tête-à-tête but we do happen to be fighting some rather aggressive chappies out there. If you girls must play such dramatic scenes do them from a safer place.'

Brit swung round and fired at the men who were moving back into place again, moving with such languid pace that it appeared he was bored with the whole thing. Juanita watched the young man as if she could hardly believe her eyes. '*Who* is that?' she gasped.

In a voice equally low Gloria replied, 'The man I'm going to marry.'

'Lot of coming and going out there, Doc, old chap,' Brit remarked, as lead started coming at the house again. 'Losing the tunnel's stirred them up. I think they might even start to fight again.'

Waco came into the room. He'd heard various vague sounds from under the house but did not connect them with anything. His eyes went to the Mexican girl, then to Doc, who grinned maliciously. 'She just come through the bunkhouse. Said you was asleep and didn't like to wake you.'

'Yeah,' Waco did not appear to be too worried. 'What was all the noise I heard?'

'Waco!' Brit's voice was urgent. 'Those bally thugs are riding around in a circle out of rifle range. I think they may be trying to outflank us.'

'Right!' Waco turned, then halted at the door. 'What's a thug?'

'Members of an old Indian murder cult.'

'Ain't one of them out there, only S Star,' Waco whooped, then he was gone.

'Miss Estradre, would you go to the bunkhouse and load for Waco. I think he's going to be busy.'

'He's harmless, Neety, you'll be safe,' Gloria went on.

Juanita left and Gloria joined Brit at the window. He leaned the rifle out and fired twice, drawing a scattering of shots back. Ducking down he sat on the floor beside the girl and handed her his rifle to reload. Taking up the second weapon he remarked: 'You know old gal, I don't know which sounds best. The Countess of Hawksden or just plain Mrs. Brit.'

Gloria shoved bullets into the loading slot of the Winchester. She had almost finished when the meaning of the words hit her. Swinging round she gasped, 'What did you say. Oh Brit. I've got to tell Neety.'

She started to get to her feet but he caught her arm and dragged her down again. 'Easy, old girl. There's some shooting going on.'

Waco lounged by the window of the bunkhouse room when Juanita came in. 'Howdy ma'am, you got tired and headed home again?'

'No, why?'

'This's the way you came in,' he glanced out of the window. 'Say, just look at these four there, sneaking up here after us.'

Juanita joined the young man at the window, looking out to where four S Star men were darting forward on foot, making for whatever cover they could find towards the forge and the bunkhouse. 'What about them? Like ole Brit says, have to dissuade them. They reckon they're real smart ole Injuns. Watch that one.'

Waco came up fast, his rifle cracking. A man sneaking towards the shelter of the forge gave a howl as a bullet cut a furrow under his feet. He took a flying dive which brought him to safety an instant after his friends landed.

By now the S Star guns were surrounding the KH house, their rifles crashing out from wherever they could find a place to take cover. It was a long range fight, for those men held the accuracy of KH too highly to make any pitched attack. Bullets sobbed, and screamed off with a banshee wail of ricochets, but for all of that they did not manage to hit the KH crew, all keeping back out of sight and letting S

Star waste lead.

Up in Painthoss's room Red Blaze grinned at the old-timer and fired down into the woods. 'Looks like shaping up into a fair old fight. Bet you wish you was in it.'

Painthoss gave a howl which sounded like the mating call of a razor-back hog. 'You no-good, red-haired wart. Just you wait, I'll——'

'There's a gent down there, can see him real plain, he's got a Sharp's buffalo gun and pouring lead out like he don't have to pay for it.'

'You couldn't hit him from here with that rusted ole relic,' Painthoss scoffed, eyeing Red's old Spencer in disgust.

'Naw?' Red hefted the gun and eared back the big side hammer. 'She ain't a bad gun. All I have to do is line her up real careful, like so.' He rested the gun on the window-sill. The gunmen were concentrating their fire on the downstairs now and the man with the buffalo gun was exposed to him. 'Make allowance for the wind, for the drop in the bullet, like so. Press the trigger and——'

A dull, dry click sounded to his ears and Red's face flushed scarlet. He'd committed the classic blunder. He had not counted his shots. Looking at the highly delighted Painthoss, he shrugged, took up some more Spencer bullets and slid them into the butt magazine. Then he lined again and pulled the trigger. The Spencer was a short range weapon and even at two hundred yards was getting to an unreliable point. The bullet came close enough to the man to make him swing back out of his hiding place. From below in the sitting-room Brit's rifle cracked and the man spun round, then dropped.

'Get him?' Painthoss asked.

'Naw, the range's too much.'

'Got me a Spencer rifle.'

'That'll reach him,' Red answered eagerly. 'Where is she?'

'Over to home, but you'll have to fetch her.'

Red grinned at the old-timer. 'Thanks, I'll decline. Anyways, it's what I'd expect of you, Injun-giver.'

Downstairs Brit lowered his rifle after dropping the man Red flushed out for him. Then he saw a white rag waving on the end of a rifle. A man came walking from behind the corral.

'KH!' the man yelled. 'You hear me?'

'I hear you!' Brit answered.

'We've got a charge of dynamite in the tunnel. Reckon it's under the house. You come on out or we'll set her off.'

CHAPTER FIFTEEN

DUSTY'S FRIENDS

RENE HAMILTON stood swaying, the world roaring before her eyes, hardly seeing Lanton, the banker, the sheriff, his deputy, Willet or the preacher. She felt the cold gold of the ring on her finger and a shudder ran through her. She was married to that fat, loathsome man. The door of the room opened. Lanton did not turn, for it would be one of the two deputies who'd been left outside to guard the house.

'You'll make a right becoming widow, Rene.'

No sound in the world had ever been so sweet to Rene's ears as those soft drawled words, spoken in the voice of Dusty Fog.

The two young Texans stood just inside the room. From the open door an arm lay in view. It belonged to the deputy Dusty had dealt with. The other was not so fortunate. He'd tried to fight against Mark Counter's powerful hands and now lay stiffening, with a broken neck.

For an instant Lanton and the others stood still. Mark's eyes on Snag Willet, a cold flat smile on his face. Lanton recovered first, his hand lashing up and across his body, under his coat to the butt of the Webley Bulldog gun. 'Kill 'em,' he screamed.

Dusty and Mark separated, one going either way. With a hiss of triumph Dusty's bone handled guns were out and roaring. The right hand gun sent bullet after bullet into Lanton's fat body, the left throwing lead into the gunman with the deputy's badge.

An instant behind Dusty's matched guns Mark was in action, cutting down Snag Willet while that killer's hands were only clamping on his gun butts. The sheriff threw down on Mark, missing him by an hairsbreadth and then Lynch was going over backwards with a ·45 bullet in his chest.

Rene stood as if she was paralysed but the preacher was wise in the ways of corpse and cartridge affairs like this. He caught the girl's arm and dragged her to the floor, holding her down while overhead the thunder of guns shattered the room and powder smoke laid down swirling eddies. She saw a gun land by her side, then the sheriff's body landed across her legs.

The banker was trying to line his gun on Mark Counter when Dusty swung his left hand gun and fired. Ames screamed as lead tore through his shoulder. He reeled backwards and tripped, then stayed down screaming for the Texans not to kill him.

Lanton reeled under the impact of the bullets, his huge frame taking the lead and absorbing the shock. His gun crashed back as fast as he could handle the trigger. Dusty's hat tore from his head, and he felt as if a red hot iron was pressed against his thigh as a Webley bullet tore his levis and gave a flesh wound. Only the rocking impact of the Colt's bullets saved Dusty's life. Lanton was shooting through the smoke and at the crouching, deadly figure from which spurts of flame tore and brought fresh agony to the huge, gross man.

Reeling like a drunken man—Lanton saw Rene looking up at him, her eyes filled with loathing. Something snapped in his mind. This was the woman who'd brought him to an end. It was through her he was dying here. Ignoring Dusty —he tried to bring the gun down to line on Rene.

The preacher caught up Lynch's gun, holding it in both hands and pulling the hammer back and firing. The bullet went up under Lanton's jaw, smashing up through the top of the man's head. For a moment Lanton stood erect, then he crashed down on to the fainting girl.

Dusty leaped forward, rolling the body from Rene, ignoring the pain in his leg. He knew the wound was not dangerous or he wouldn't be standing on his leg.

All was silent, the smoke blowing from the open door. Lanton and his men were done, only Ames remaining alive. 'Don't kill me,' he screamed. 'Don't——'

Mark dragged the man up. 'Did Lanton touch her?'
'No. Honestly. Don't hurt me.'
With a contemptuous shove Mark hurled the man aside. 'If he'd touched Rene I'd have killed you.'
Gently the preacher and Dusty lifted the girl up, it was some seconds before she opened her eyes. Then she threw her arms round Dusty's neck, sobbing hysterically. Gently Dusty thrust her from him as he heard men running forward.
'Dusty!' It was Henery of the Eating House and the owner of the telegraph office who entered. 'What happened?'
Rene looked up. Mark came towards her as the preacher talked gently to her. 'Were they married?'
'Yes, but I think it can be declared void, due to the way it was brought about.'
'Yeah,' Mark took the girl's hand, 'Listen, honey. He's dead now. That means, as his widow, you own a fair piece of range. The S Star and some of the Lazy F.'
'I want nothing of his,' Rene answered, taking the ring off and throwing it to the floor.
'Waal now.You look at it this way. You and Just's going to need more room. There ain't going to be all that much room at the KH when both families start growing.'
'Just!' Rene came to her feet, her eyes wild. 'Just, he's in the next room.'
Mark watched the girl run from the room, then glanced at Dusty who was pulling the watch from Lanton's vest. 'Load up, Mark. We're headed for the KH before it's too late.'
Henery looked at Dusty for a moment, then said, 'Cap'n Fog, I forgot. There are a lot of really good guns in town. They're at the saloon. They must be waiting for Lanton.'
Shoving the watch into his torn levis Dusty started to load his guns. Henery went upstairs and came back with strips of sheet. He bandaged Dusty's leg and sent the other man to fetch a new pair of levis from the store.
Dusty and Mark went and looked into the next room. Rene and Just were locked in each other's arms, oblivious of everything. Mark closed the door again. 'Don't approve of a young widow acting like that,' he said.

With the new levis on Dusty started for the door. Henery asked, 'What do you aim to do?'

'Go along to the saloon.'

At the KH Brit looked at the others. One thought in every mind. Was what the S Star man saying true?

'Look!' Gloria gasped, pointing to the ford. A group of hard riding men came tearing around into sight. 'More of them.'

Winter saw the new men and thought nothing of it. He'd heard rumours of gunmen gathering in town and wondered if Lanton hired them to help here.

The riders tore in between Winter's men and the KH and swung their horses to halt, facing the S Star gunmen. It was then Winter recognised the small man on the tired looking horse, and the huge, handsome blond giant who sat next to him. Others of the men were looking along the line and muttering amongst themselves as they recognised this or that man.

'Lanton's dead!'

Dusty looked down at Winters as he spoke. The gunman did not make a move. 'That right?'

'Sure, here's his watch.' Dusty tossed the watch down before the man. 'You wanting to carry on with this?'

'Maybe.'

'I'd better introduce my friends. Then if you still want, you can cut loose your wolves and we'll see the way they fight.'

Dusty jerked his thumb back over his shoulder, pointing first to the squat, hard looking man at the end of the line, then moving along. It was like a roll call of the honour students of border gunplay.

'Ben Thompson, Billy Thompson, Kin Fisher, Bill Longley, Clay Allison, Shad and Mannen Cements, Wes Hardin, Jim Courtwright, Dallas Stoudenmire, Cheyenne Bodie, Bronco Layne.'

Winter looked along the line of hard-eyed men. Some of them he knew, the others were as Dusty named them. They were the cream of the fast men, almost everyone wearing a Gaylin gunbelt. They were a bunch it would be hard to take.

'Before you make your decision look over there,' Mark went on.

Winter looked to where hard riding vaqueros were fast approaching; led by Don Jose Estradre and a black dressed boy who rode a sorrel but had a huge white stallion running loose by his side.

'Lanton's dead!' the gunman said softly.

'I killed him in town.'

Turning, Winter waved to the other men. 'All right. Let's get out of here. There's nothing to fight over now.'

The KH crew came from the house, Brit and Gloria running towards Dusty and Mark. Waco, Doc and Red came forward to greet their friends in the line of Dusty's amigos. Juanita Estradre ran to her father, throwing her arms round his neck as he swung down from his horse.

With his arm around Gloria's shoulder Brit looked at the others, then called for them to come to the house. The S Star hired killers were riding away. Lanton was dead and peace was on the land.

There would be no more need for guns on the Azul Rio.

THE END